A Yooper's Summer on Isle Royale

A YOOPER'S SUMMER on ISLE ROYALE

Dan Kemp

iUniverse, Inc.
Bloomington

A Yooper's Summer on Isle Royale

iUniverse books may be ordered through booksellers or by contacting:

iUniverse
1663 Liberty Drive
Bloomington, IN 47403
www.iuniverse.com
1-800-Authors (1-800-288-4677)

ISBN: 978-1-4759-8439-2 (sc)
ISBN: 978-1-4759-8440-8 (hc)
ISBN: 978-1-4759-8441-5 (e)

Library of Congress Control Number: 2013906189

Printed in the United States of America

iUniverse rev. date: 04/16/2013

This book is dedicated to my wife, Joan Kemp. *A Yooper's Summer on Isle Royale* would not have happened if it wasn't for the "motivational" urging and encouragement from her.

Preface

I have been telling these stories for decades and stopped counting the times I heard, "You should write a book." Here it is.

If it wasn't for our endless supply of lawyers and suers who employ them, I could have made some changes and proclaimed this non fiction. *A Yooper's Summer on Isle Royale* is based on some true events; however, all persons appearing in this work are fictitious. Any resemblance to real people, living or dead is an amazing coincidence.

There are a couple of words in the title that are foreign for the uninitiated. A Yooper is a title worn with pride by those of us who grew up in Michigan's Upper Peninsula- the U.P- making us UPers. The internet is resplendent with definitions of "Yooper" and the New York Times devoted a long article some years ago trying to capture the essence of being a Yooper.

The other foreign word on the cover is "sisu." It is the Finnish term for what ever comes after you have used up all of your courage, perseverance, and bulldog tenacity. Sisu was a by-product of growing up in the U.P. When you have winters with over 300 inches of snow, spring black flies with teeth, summer mosquitoes with measurable wingspans, and snow on the Fourth of July, you need sisu to survive. There was a reason some of the early maps labeled the Upper Peninsula "uninhabitable."

Do not confuse sisu with stupidity, as you will find liberal doses of both in these pages. I really did cross about 100 miles of Lake Superior, from Copper Harbor, Michigan to Thunder Bay, Ontario, in a 14 foot boat. This is one of the best examples of stupidity and sisu. I will leave it to you to distinguish the others.

For those unfamiliar with Isle Royale, it is our only island National Park. It is one of the most beautiful places I have ever been. Ben Franklin helped broker a deal with the French to include Isle Royale as part of the United States even though it is closer to Canada. Michigan received Isle Royale as part of the deal with Ohio. Ohio got a 10 mile strip of land from southern Michigan, which included Toledo, in return for the Upper Peninsula and Isle Royale. Thank you, Ben.

I am not sure how much luck each of us is allotted, but I left a big chunk of mine on Isle Royale.

Acknowledgements

Thanks to Jerry Farmer who gave me a historical perspective of the Island and Rock Harbor Lodge before Isle Royale was a National Park. Jerry's family ran Rock Harbor Lodge and the resort on Belle Isle until the Park Service took over. Thanks to the National Park Service who gave me permission to use their map to give some context to the locations I describe, the cover illustrator, Cole Denver Peterson of Cole Denver Designs, to Nora Heikkinen who showed me why I should have paid more attention in Mrs. Wilson's English class, and to Pete Oikarainen for help and encouragement.

Contents

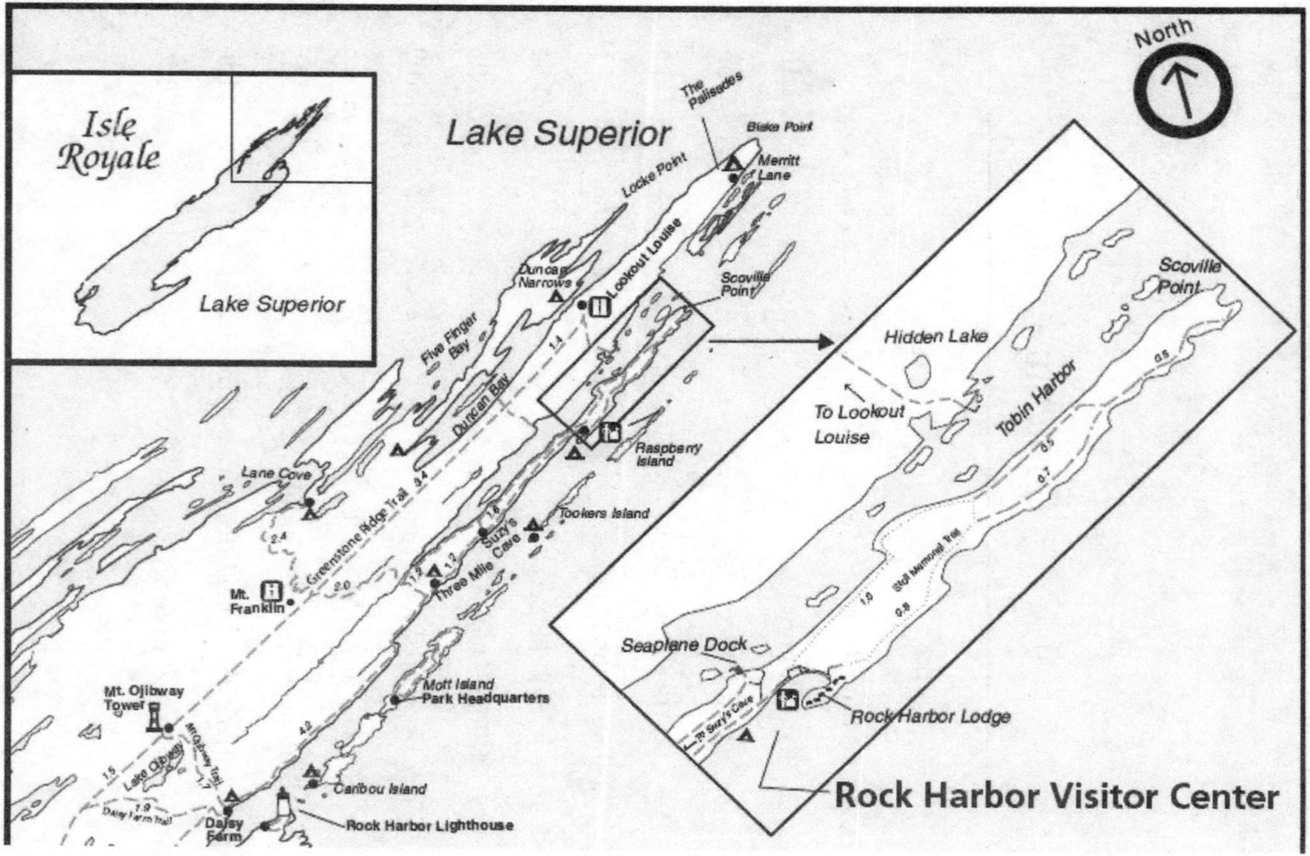
North
Isle Royale
Lake Superior
Lake Superior
The Palisades
Blake Point
Merritt Lane
Locke Point
Lookout Louise
Duncan Narrows
Scoville Point
Five Finger Bay
Duncan Bay
Raspberry Island
Lane Cove
Greenstone Ridge Trail
Tookers Island
Suzy's Cave
Three Mile
Mt. Franklin
Mott Island
Park Headquarters
Mt. Ojibway Tower
Mt. Ojibway Trail
Lake Ojibway
Daisy Farm Trail
Daisy Farm
Caribou Island
Rock Harbor Lighthouse
Hidden Lake
To Lookout Louise
Tobin Harbor
Scoville Point
Stoll Memorial Trail
Seaplane Dock
Rock Harbor Lodge
Rock Harbor Visitor Center

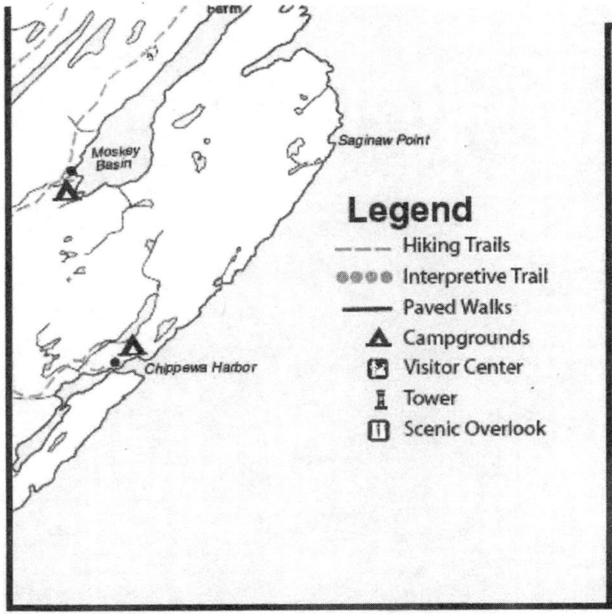
Moskey Basin
Saginaw Point
Chippewa Harbor
Legend
Hiking Trails
Interpretive Trail
Paved Walks
Campgrounds
Visitor Center
Tower
Scenic Overlook

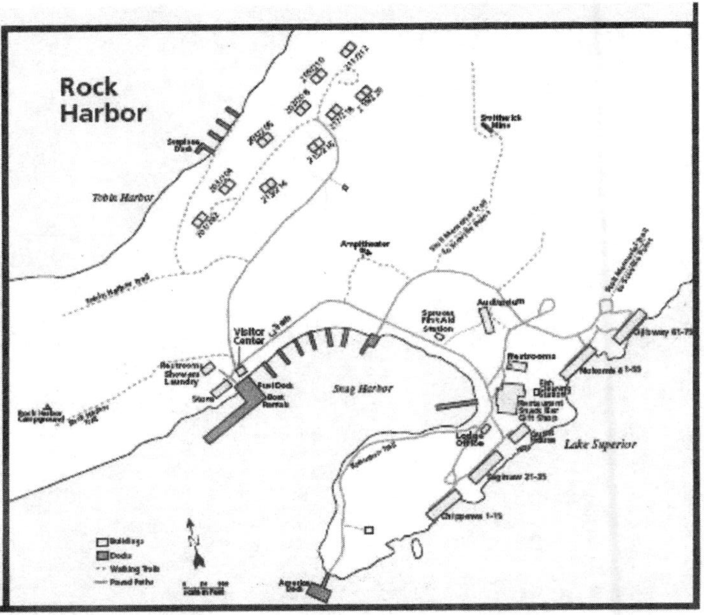
Rock Harbor
Tobin Harbor
Visitor Center
Snug Harbor
Lake Superior
Restrooms
Auditorium
Chippewa 1-15
Saginaw 21-35

A YOOPER'S SUMMER
on
ISLE ROYALE

Chapter 1

GETTING THERE

"Rested on an Island,
On an island green and grassy,
Yonder in the big sea water."
Hiawatha

We didn't anticipate any problems. Digger and I checked the weather reports, wind reports, NOAA broadcasts, and Coast Guard reports for June sixth through June ninth. Nothing led us to believe the weather was pause for thought. We were ready as anyone could be to cross Lake Superior in a fourteen foot aluminum boat. Never mind it was probably the smallest boat to cross since the fur trappers made John Jacob Astor rich. The Big Lake has claimed hundreds of vessels of all sizes and has spawned harrowing tales from those that survived. When you're nineteen years old, there is no doubt in your mind that you are going to be one of the survivors.

The risks of crossing the Big Lake go way beyond most bodies of water. The weather is hard to predict as Lake Superior can create its own weather due to its size, geographic location, and water temperature. Storms and winds can occur almost instantly. In early June, the water temperature is in the mid-thirties which presents additional risks. If the waves are high enough, an open boat will quickly fill with water and the spray will cause hypothermia. If you happen to capsize, your life expectancy can be measured in minutes.

I didn't tell Digger, but I thought the crossing was a hair brained idea from the get go. I got put in a corner after I let my mouth overload my ass. It all happened when we were sitting around the lounge at Michigan Tech, talking about everything and nothing. I just bought a new boat and in one of those insane moments, said that I wouldn't be afraid to take it across the Big Lake. That is not what you want to say in front of an all-pro cast of ball busters. By the time they were through with me, I was reverting to my fifth grade retorts; "Yeah, you'll see. I WILL take her across."

One of the two people we told about the crossing, Carl, drove us to the boat launch at Copper Harbor. The other person we told was a local undertaker and a shirt-tail relative of Digger's. He made us leave a note in his hallway that he could "find" in the morning, after we were well underway. There was no way he wanted to have this information in time to stop us, in case we didn't make it.

Our payload consisted of a spare fifteen horsepower Evinrude motor, fishing gear, five cases of beer, six bottles of cheap whiskey, seventeen gallons of mixed gas, sandwiches, and winter clothes. The whiskey and beer were mostly for resale on the Island. When we put the boat in the water, there wasn't much freeboard, so we decided to leave the spare motor with Carl. He said he would put the motor on one of the passenger boats in the next week or two. There still wasn't a lot of free board, but there wasn't anything else we could leave behind.

Oh yeah, there were also two yahoos: Digger (John Ojala), who came by his nickname because his father was an undertaker; and me, Wayne Kallio. The ball busters called me "RH" for Rock Head. My last name, Kallio, translated from Finnish into English is Rock.

Digger and I pushed off from Copper Harbor, Michigan at five in the morning, on June 6th, 1965, bound for Isle Royale National Park almost fifty miles away, in the middle of Lake Superior. Our boat looked a lot smaller than ever before.

We were on our way to our summer jobs and decided to cross the Big Lake mostly for bragging rights and double dare. My employment letter outlined a few of my duties as a bell-hop and salary. I would be making twenty-nine dollars a month plus room and board. At this rate, February is the only month I would have been able to make a dollar a day, but the Island is closed for the winter.

A few Lake Superior factoids: You could put the other four great lakes (Michigan, Huron, Erie, and Ontario) in Lake Superior and still have room for three more Lake Eries. The water in Superior could cover the forty-eight contiguous states in almost six feet of water. The average yearly temperature twenty feet down is thirty-eight degrees. The average depth of Superior is nearly five hundred feet. You can put four New Jerseys into the Big Lake and still have room for Rhode Island. Isle Royale is farther north than Maine, Quebec, Nova Scotia, and most of the population of Canada.

I am having second thoughts. It had been just seven years since the sinking of the Carl D. Bradley where thirty-three of thirty-five sailors lost their lives, and the stories of the sinking were still fresh in my mind. Although the Bradley went down in Lake Michigan, the same storm made converts of most of the sailors on Lake Superior that day. The waves were thirty feet high and the winds were seventy miles an hour with gusts approaching ninety. The Bradley was the largest boat on the lakes at 623 feet, until the title was lost to the Edmund Fitzgerald at 729 feet, which was launched the same year the Bradley went down.

One of the guys who shipped on the Fitzgerald during that maiden season said he saw seasoned sailors genuinely afraid and praying during the storm that sank the Bradley. All of these things were on my mind. Digger just shrugged, "Ya gotta take some chances in this life."

As kids, we dreamed about going to the island. I will never forget an article in "Outdoor Life" magazine that detailed a fishing expedition to the Island. The author talked about inland lakes he fished and was convinced that he was the only one to fish them that summer. He went into savory detail about how he caught a northern pike on every cast! The Island would have been teeming with fishermen if it wasn't such a tough place to get to. It takes a full day to drive from Chicago or Detroit to one of the boat launch points. Then, it is most of another day to get to the Island. Finally, you need another day to get to one of the inland lakes by foot. Here we were, about to spend the summer on this magical place that I had dreamed about all my dreamable life.

The Upper Peninsula (U.P.) of Michigan is one of the most remote areas in the United States. The nearest traffic light was one hundred-fifteen miles from our house. The entire Keweenaw County had less than four people per square mile and only one law officer in the entire county. The phone book had one page for all of Keweenaw County and not all of the letters in the alphabet were used.

There has always been tension between the two peninsulas of Michigan. The folks from the Lower Peninsula mostly used the Upper Peninsula as a vacation spot and over the years, we became "UPers," which evolved into Yoopers. The Lower Peninsula folks thought they were being derogatory, and, in true Yooper style, we adopted the name proudly. Because of the remoteness, Yoopers feel a special kinship to one another and we all consider the U.P. as the biggest geographic fraternity in the country.

The U.P. is not connected to Lower Michigan except by the five mile long Mackinaw Bridge. The Lower Peninsula inhabitants became "trolls" because they lived below the bridge. There has been a proposal on the table since the Mackinaw Bridge was built to add a trap door on the north bound lanes which would be activated as soon as the U.P. seceded from Michigan.

As late as 1837, the year Michigan was admitted to the Union, a federal report described the U.P. as "a sterile region on the shores of Lake Superior destined by soil and climate to forever remain a wilderness." There are some people that still hold to this premise. Michigan and Ohio were embroiled in a border dispute about a ten mile strip of land on the Michigan/Ohio border. President Andrew Jackson and Congress pressured the Michigan territory to accept the Upper Peninsula in return for the ten mile strip, which included Toledo.

Ohio was sure they got the better of the deal until copper, iron ore, and vast timber resources were discovered in the U.P. several years later. At one time, the U.P. supplied ninety percent of the United States' copper; most of its iron ore and the lumber built the cities in Lower Michigan. The U.P. produced more mineral wealth than the California gold rush.

Most of us Yoopers were poor, but we didn't know it. I always had an allowance growing up which consisted of being "allowed" to keep any money I earned by cutting grass or shoveling snow.

I was looking to buy a couple of outboard motors and happened to mention it to Bill Koskela. Bill Koskela was a boat pilot on the Island who also worked for the same company that hired me; the National Park Concessions (NPC). Bill told me that

Piggy Lambert, the owner of Lac La Belle's boat, motor, sales, and service had a bunch of used motors.

Lac La Belle is a lake and small settlement almost as far north as you can go in the State of Michigan without a boat. In fact, it is about sixteen miles south of the sign in a cul-de-sac that proclaims, "US 41 ENDS."

I went there in March when the path to the front door to Piggy's was cut in the snow and was still higher than my head. That was what was left of our three hundred thirty inches of snow that winter.

The front of the building was lined with aluminum boats on end that were covered half way up with snow. Besides being for sale, I think they were used to keep snow away from the wooden siding.

I walked in the front door and the entire floor was littered with outboard motors. "Nice to meet you, Mr. Lambert."

"Just call me Piggy." Nicknames, even the harshest ones in the Yoop are an affirmation that you are liked and can take a ribbing.

There was no guessing how Piggy got his nickname. He had a huge belly that he hid beneath his bib overalls. He had his pants hiked so high, he really didn't need a shirt. He could have just cut armholes in his pockets.

"Well Piggy, I need a couple of reliable outboards in the fifteen to twenty horsepower range. I am going to be on Isle Royale all summer and getting them fixed may not be an option." The reason I wanted two motors was that the dock attendant from the year before told me there were never enough motors to rent out. I figured I could make enough to pay for both motors by renting mine when the National Park Concessions (licensed renter of boats and motors) ran out of motors. The NPC would never sanction this, but the person in charge of boat and motor rentals this year was Digger.

Piggy scanned the inventory and pointed out an eighteen horse Johnson and a fifteen horse Evinrude. Both were about five years old and in perfect shape, swore Piggy.

"How much for both?" I asked.

Piggy did his best imitation of mentally calculating the price and said "five hundred forty- five dollars for both."

I was at the mercy of Piggy's assessment of the motors. Five hundred forty-five dollars was a lot of money when you are making one dollar and sixty cents an hour at the local grocery store and eight dollars a week shoveling snow every day. Another point of perspective: a new Ford Mustang had a list price of around eighteen hundred dollars.

I was able to save enough from shoveling snow that winter to buy my fourteen foot Starcraft outright; but, I didn't have any money left to buy a motor. I believe there is no where but the Upper Peninsula of Michigan where a nineteen-year-old with no money could even think about buying an outboard motor on his own, much less buy two motors.

I said, "I'll take 'em, and I can give you twenty bucks to hold them until I get more money."

Piggy said, "It's a deal. Grab the Evinrude and we'll put 'em in your car."

I was surprised, but Piggy assured me he didn't have the space to store them. We walked back to the shop and I stood at the counter waiting for Piggy to complete the paper work. I stood there for a while and asked Piggy if he was going to prepare a bill.

"I don't believe in paper work and anyhow, I don't have the time or space to monkey around with all that paper," Piggy explained. "You owe me five hundred twenty-five dollars; what else do you need to know?"

"What happens if I don't pay you?" I asked.

"Well son, if you decide not to pay me, a piece of paper isn't going to change much. Besides, if you don't pay me, you will be the first one not to. If you can live with that, so can I." I don't think Piggy even remembered my name. Only in the U.P.!

The snow and ice on Lac LaBelle and the Big Lake finally melted. Bill Koskela had a camp not far from Piggy's shop and let me keep my boat at his dock. Bill was a retired Superintendant of Schools turned boat captain. Bill always morphed into the character he happened to be at the time. When he spoke about his teaching career, he took on the role of a teacher; when he talked about being a boat captain, he took on the character of someone that never made it through eighth grade. Also, there wasn't a single sentence that didn't contain some profanity no matter what role he was playing or who was around.

We made a few shakedown trips to try to get an estimate of how much gas we would need and how to load the boat in case of heavy seas, but nothing can prepare you for a trip across Lake Superior. On one of those shakedowns, I traveled about ten miles along the coast of the Big Lake to the mouth of a river that was only accessible by foot or by boat. I still hadn't gotten around to getting a boat license, and was on my way back from the short fishing junket when a small boat shot out from behind a rock formation, trying to intercept me. Fortunately, the would-be interceptor had a smaller motor than mine and I steered wide at full throttle.

As I looked back to see who this lunatic was, I saw a uniformed guy holding what appeared to be a badge. I stayed on the throttle and was beginning to put some distance between me and the badge. I figured it was a conservation officer who was probably watching me fish. Not only did I not have a boat license, I also didn't have a fishing license, life jackets, or running lights. I guess you could add resisting arrest to that list.

Now, Captain Courageous replaced the badge with a pistol. He was screaming and waving the pistol. I positioned the gas tank further forward to get a mile-or-two per hour more speed. Captain Courageous started firing the pistol. Hopefully, they were warning shots. I sat on the floor of the boat and tried to keep the motor between Captain Courageous and my head. I was getting close to the inlet of Lac La Belle and I could see the commercial fishermen had just returned from pulling their nets. They were all standing on the dock next to the sign that said "NO WAKE – 5 MILES PER HOUR."

The boys were hollering and shaking their fists as I blew by wide open. They didn't realize that Captain Courageous was in hot pursuit. It was another three miles to Lac La Belle where I kept my boat and I began thinking about how I was going to hide a fourteen foot boat in a rather small lake. By the time I reached the dock where I launched from, I had about a two mile lead on Captain Courageous and it was almost dark. Bill Koskela's dock wasn't visible from the channel to Lake Superior, which meant you had to be in Lac La Belle to see it. Bill had his boat on one side of the dock and I was using the other side. I noticed that there was a narrow space between the deck and the water, and I was able to push my boat under the dock right next to Bill's. Bill's boat acted as a shield and the only way you could see my boat was if you got next to the dock and looked underneath. Besides, it didn't look like a boat would fit underneath the dock.

I figured Captain Courageous would call or radio for help, so I jumped in my car and headed for home. There was a public boat ramp in Lac La Belle, and by the time Captain Courageous got there, he must have assumed I loaded my boat on a trailer and left. As I got closer to home, there was a State Police car coming at me, going like the hammers of hell.

I decided to name the Starcraft, the *Sisu,* which is Finnish for whatever comes after courage ends. Sisu is what takes over when a Finn is battling overwhelming odds and doesn't allow him to quit. All four of my grandparents came from Finland and so did Digger's, so *Sisu* only seemed fitting.

We were ready to put our sisu and the *Sisu* to the test. Carl pushed us away from the Copper Harbor Marina dock and it was game-on!

The clarity of the water in Superior never fails to amaze me. As we drifted from the dock in Copper Harbor, you could see the rocks at the bottom about twenty feet down. As I looked out at the open sea, the blueness of the water beckoned, and seemed to say, "No problem - come on out." Rough water is only part of the danger the Big Lake poses. If you capsize at this time of year, you may be able to live for forty-five minutes, life jacket or no life jacket, provided you keep your shoes on.

Hypothermia is an ever present threat. Body heat is lost more quickly in water than on land. Water temperatures that would be quite reasonable as outdoor air temperatures can lead to hypothermia. A water temperature of fifty degrees Fahrenheit (F) often leads to death in one hour, and water temperatures hovering at freezing can lead to death in as little as fifteen minutes.

I was really feeling the butterflies in my stomach, knowing we were locked into this fool's journey.

We both had winter coats and hats, but I had forgotten to wear long-johns and our boat quickly turned into a fourteen foot meat locker with an outboard motor. The weather report held true, except that the air temperature dipped below freezing during the night. Since the Big Lake is close to 32° F in early June, a thin sheet of ice formed on the calm water overnight. The morning breeze and currents gathered the ice into windrows which were one to two foot piles, miles wide. We didn't find this out until we were at least ten miles from shore.

There is a reason they make pots and beer cans out of aluminum. Not only do they transmit heat exceedingly well, they do the same thing with cold. Besides the water being ice cold, so was the air. Coupled with our forward motion, we generated our own wind chill factor and we instantly became colder than a Mother-in-law's love.

The ice slowed the boat to a crawl and the motor was limping. With forty or so miles to go, we saw what looked like a tidal wave ahead. Perhaps worse, it was a fog bank so dense that as we entered, we couldn't see past the bow of the boat.

The air temperature, water temperature, and humidity were conducive to an advection fog, also known as "sea fog." An advection fog can occur when an air mass moves over a large body of water that is cooler or warmer than the water. In this case, the air was cooler than the Big Lake and resulted in an enormous fog bank.

Suddenly, we had two problems: a seemingly impenetrable fog we couldn't see through and ice we couldn't plow through. We were going so slow, Digger broke out the oars and tried to help the motor through the ice. The only thing this accomplished was to snap one of the oars, which left us with one jagged harpoon and an oar. Rowing with one oar struck me as a cruel metaphor describing this venture.

In our planning sessions, Digger volunteered to bring a compass and act as navigator. He said he saw his dad navigate on the Big Lake many times and knew how. Because of the fog, we had no idea where we were going. It was time for the compass, which resulted in problem three. The compass Digger brought was a plastic imitation Boy Scout compass that he did not know how to read.

I could read it, but the compass had to be held perfectly flat to let the needle rotate freely. I finally got the compass flat, but the needle was still gyrating wildly. We finally figured out that it was the magneto in the motor creating a magnetic field that drove the needle crazy. So, you had to either get out of the boat, or shut down the motor and steady the compass on the ice chest lid to read it. By the time the needle swung around, the boat was pointed in a different direction.

Since we weren't dealing with a military grade compass here, we established a compass reading routine. As soon as I shut the motor off, Digger would pick out a piece of ice about ten feet from the bow which was about as far ahead as we could see. Digger would then point like a bird dog until I could get a reading and make a course adjustment.

Problem four: The 33° F water made the motor hard to restart, so we had to keep the compass readings to a minimum. Without the motor, death was a certainty. It was during these shut downs that I hoped Piggy wasn't bull-shitting about the quality of the motor. Any reservations I had about the crossing were trumped by Digger's exclamation, "Hell, ya gotta take some chances in this life."

During one of the shut downs, we heard a fog horn which made all of our other problems seem small. It wasn't hard to figure that since we were miles from shore, the fog horn had to belong to an ore boat. Strange, they should call an eight-hundred-foot vessel a boat. We had a boat. It is also strange to me that they name all of the freighters on the Great Lakes after men. Since we couldn't tell where the ship was, we decided to stay as close to our position with the motor idling. Hopefully, the ore boat's radar could pinpoint our boat and give them enough time to miss us.

The fog horn was getting closer, and we started to question our decision. Then, the ore boat blew a warning signal, which sounded like he was on top of us. At least he saw us. It takes a lot of water to turn one of those boats and even more when they are loaded. Digger and I decided to open a beer, since there wasn't time to fix our last meal. The sound of the engine was on us and the terrifying part was not being able to see anything.

We knew he was close because his bow wake was coming right at us. They looked like four footers, and two feet of the wave was made up of mostly ice. The waves broke over our bow leaving us soaking wet with a foot of ice water in the bottom of the boat. The good news: the ore boat didn't hit us.

We were both soaked to the skin with 33° F water. My teeth were chattering like those windup Halloween toys. Even though Digger did remember his long-johns, he wasn't faring much better. They were kind of acting like a poor man's wet suit. Our situation went from scary to dire. Hypothermia became problem five and I decided to suspend numbering the problems. Navigating became a joke. I could have done as well with a gunny sack over my head.

For the next three hours we plowed ice and took compass readings as best we could. The cold was beginning to take its toll. I kept telling myself that it was June - like that would automatically make it warmer. It is a fact that Finns have more hair on the north side of their bodies, but even at that it ain't much and certainly not enough to add any warmth. At one point, the nukku (Finnish for 'sleep') monster got me and it felt so good, it took Digger slapping my face to startle me awake. Finally, the ice age ended, but the fog was still on us like a tent.

Then, just as suddenly as the fog appeared, it disappeared. The waves picked up a little, but at least we could see we were in the middle of the Lake. The fog bank was behind us and hopefully the Island was ahead of us.

I was fighting to keep my eyes open and we took turns slapping each other to stay awake. I think I know how that guy on the Santa Maria felt when he first saw the Canary Islands. The mountains on the Island were finally visible; based on the topography, we were only about twenty miles off-course. The highest point on the Island is about fourteen hundred feet high, so the island is visible a long way out. If we didn't fall asleep, we had a chance of making it. We had to steer to the northeast as our destination was Rock Harbor on the very northeast end of the Island.

Nothing prepares you for the sight of the Island as you approach from any direction by sea or air. The water is so clear and cold, it is unimaginable there is that much pure water left on earth. Seeing the greenness mixed with rock coming right to the water's edge and competing with the crystal clear blue water for space is why God gave us memories. No matter how many times I went to the Island, that first glimpse gives you the feeling that you are about to land in a magical place. And, indeed we were.

Seven and a half hours after leaving Copper Harbor, we pulled into Rock Harbor. I felt like Patton rolling into Paris after liberating France. Instead of being greeted by adoring throngs, there was John Haapala, a retired fishermanand current boat pilot, painting one of the rental scows, and one Smokey (a National Park Ranger wearing his Smokey the Bear hat), who turned out to be the real life Dudley Dooright.

"I am going to have to impound your boat," said Dudley (Robert Davies), as soon as introductions were finished. Luckily, we had stashed the contraband beer and liquor on a small outer island before making our grand entrance.

"On what grounds are you impounding our vessel?" asked an indignant Digger.

"On the grounds that you took an undersized craft across Lake Superior," replied Dudley Dooright.

"I guess you are gonna have to show me that rule, since the only ones I know about only require a registration and life jackets," I said to Dudley.

Dudley didn't look too sure of himself at this point, and said, since we weren't going anywhere, he said he would have time to research the laws.

As we were unloading our gear, Jim Kangas, the head Smokey for Rock Harbor came down to introduce himself. He was not as impulsive as his underling and spent a few minutes getting to know who we were, what we were doing there, and whatever possessed us to cross the Big Lake in a fourteen foot boat. Then Jim turned to Dudley and told him he would handle it from there. Dudley stalked off, an unhappy Smokey.

I was struck by the fact that Dudley was very overweight, especially for a young guy in an outdoor occupation. His head was so big, it shaded his ears. Not his hair, his head. I chuckled at the thought of Dudley being subjected to the All Pro ball busters back in the Union building at Michigan Tech.

"Hey Smokey, I'm glad they were able to shave your fur and teach you rudimentary English."

"Hey Dudley, if you had to haul ass, it would take two trips."

"Just goes to show that God knows what he is doing; the reason he gave you such a big ass is so your head would fit."

There would be no end.

It turned out Jim, the head Smokey at Rock Harbor, was a Yooper first, Finnlander second, and a Washington-Bureaucrat a distant third. I felt an instant connection with him. It was almost like one of his job requirements was to give us hell for taking an aluminum foil tub across the Big Lake. On the other hand, I could sense some admiration from Jim for having the balls to do what we did.

The introduction to Dudley, however, was a portent of things to come. We didn't know what to expect from the Park Service. It turned out, neither did they.

Chapter 2

EARLY GOING

After our intro with the head Smokey, we went to the National Park Concession (NPC) office to check in and radio back to the mainland that we had made it. Our undertaker friend John Erickson "found" our note when he came home for lunch and had already alerted our parents, who in turn called the Park Service, so our arrival was anticipated.

Sam Burton, the NPC manager, was a real southerner from Mammoth Cave, Kentucky, and a good 'ole boy. Sam also possessed a nearly infallible bullshit detector, as I found out later. He was semi-amused that we had come across on our own; however, I felt he also looked at us like, "Uh oh. I have a couple of Yahoos on my hands." He radioed back to the office on the mainland with instructions to let our parents know we were ok.

After all of the formalities were taken care of, Sam told us where our housing would be and who we would bunk with. We asked if we could room together and he said all of the room assignments were set. I was to room with Bill Koskela. Bill was the next best roommate to Digger, as it turned out, and he would cover for me no matter what I did short of a felony. Maybe even for a small felony. There was a catch. Three guys tried to endure Bill's snoring the year before and all three were carried out on their shields. Bill was no ordinary "log sawyer." I figured I could curry a little favor with the Boss if I was able to stay in the room with Bill.

Sam figured this was a good time to go over my bellhop job duties and the rules in general. The most important job for Tom Koski, my bellhop partner, and me, was to meet every boat and plane, walk each tourist to their room, deliver their luggage, and unload all supplies for the Lodge that came in three days a week on the National Park Service (NPS) boat. In addition, we were to tend to the guests and make sure they were taken care of.

The Lodge has sixty units that resemble Holiday Inn® rooms and twenty housekeeping cabins on the ridge between Rock Harbor and Tobin Harbor. To fill the rooms and provide transportation to the campers, there were three boats and two planes that collectively required coverage seven days a week.

The NPC decided to cut the number of bell hops from four to two this year. I guess they couldn't afford the twenty nine dollars a month times four. That was fine with Tom and me as we only had to divide the tips in half and it saved a lot of possible wrangling, not to mention accounting.

There were three boats that brought tourists to Rock Harbor. The main boat was the National Park Service boat, the *Ranger III*, which sailed from Houghton, Michigan, on Monday, Wednesday, and Friday and returned to Houghton on Tuesday, Thursday, and Saturday. The *Ranger III* is 165 feet long, carries 128 passengers, and kind of looks like a shrunk down cruise ship. The *Ranger III* is the largest vessel owned by the National Park Service. The second boat, the *Isle Royale Queen II,* was owned and operated by Captain Connor and sailed six days a week from Copper Harbor, Michigan. The *Isle Royale Queen II* is 57 feet long with a capacity of 54 passengers. The *Voyageur,* which was the original *Isle Royale Queen,* sailed from Grand Portage, Minnesota on Tuesday, Thursday, and Saturday. The *Voyageur* is 40 feet long and has a capacity of 28 passengers, unless they sold more tickets. Captain Roy Olson was known to make the excess passengers members of the crew.

Two private seaplanes serviced the Island and flew every day if there were passengers. There was the Grumman *Goose*, an amphibious seaplane that was based at the airport in Hancock, Michigan, and the Twin Beechcraft, a float plane that left from National Park Headquarters on the Portage Canal in downtown Houghton, Michigan.

The Island was dry as far as tourists were concerned. This was not a National Park Service dictate, but a choice made by the National Park Concessions. Only the Park Service employees could get beer and booze via the *Ranger III* every Tuesday. The NPC had the contract to provide all tourist services from the inception of the Park in 1946. The company is headquartered in the bible belt of Kentucky and the top management boys were all direct descendants of Carrie Nation.

That is where I came in. Since Tom and I took all of the tourists to their rooms, we knew from the guys that bell-hopped the year before that the one question most asked was, "Sonny, where can a person get a drink around here?"

I had big plans to fill that void. As Henry Kaiser, founder of Kaiser Aluminum once said, "To be successful, find a need and fill it."

Tom and I met with Dave Shaw a couple of weeks before going to the Island regarding "egg shipments." Dave was the NPC mainland agent in Houghton and was responsible for getting the Lodge supplies to the Island. The plan was to hide beer in the bottom of egg cases. A thirty dozen egg carton held over four cases of beer and weighed about eighty pounds. We had to reinforce the "special" egg carton so the bottom wouldn't fall out.

Dave marked the loaded "egg" carton so that we could make sure no one but Tom carried it off the boat. Almost anyone would have a mighty struggle just picking up the case, much less carrying it to the trailer. Tom was one of the strongest guys I ever knew and he could make carrying the "egg" carton look like he was carrying a box of corn flakes. He could probably carry a Volkswagen if he could get a grip on it. We didn't call him "Lurch" for nothing.

While Digger was getting his briefing, I decided to look up Jim Kangas and thank him for saving us from Dudley.

Jim told me that most of the Smokeys at Rock Harbor were new to the Island and certainly were in for a cultural shock when they had to start dealing with Yoopers, not to mention the isolation of the Island. Isle Royale is about fifty miles from the nearest point of Michigan and Rock Harbor is almost eighty miles from the nearest point in Minnesota and forty miles from Thunder Bay, Canada, all of it by water. There was no communication available except by marine radio, and only Rock Harbor, Windigo, and Mott Island had electricity using diesel generators.

There were no TVs on the Island and the only radio station signal that made it to the Island was in Port Arthur, Canada. The reception was spotty at best.

Jim had four young Smokeys that reported directly to him. They were only a few years older than us, and this was their first assignment after getting their Bureaucrat indoctrination. I am sure none of them had ever heard of Isle Royale before this assignment and couldn't believe the isolation when they got here.

They were all single and had no access to women except for the Concession waitresses, social director, and housekeeping girls. Tourists were off-limits and they didn't have the time to court the Concession girls like we did.

Jim was from a town over one hundred thirty miles from mine, and in true Yooper fashion, we found several mutual friends and acquaintances. Forget the conventional six degrees of separation for most people on earth; Yoopers have one degree of separation. I either know or are related to someone you know, or, I am related to you.

Jim said that he could tell Dudley wasn't happy to get a reprimand in front of us and we had better be careful when dealing with him.

We walked around and met the advanced contingent for the rest of the day. It looked like we had our share of characters and three-fourths of someone else's. There was old Stan, a local with a thick Finnish accent who had to go to Windigo, on the other end of the Island. This was much to his displeasure as it was a six hour boat ride. Old Stan could not just say Windigo. Every reference to that area by Stan was "Vindigo, Kot Dam" as in "I gotta go Vindigo, Kot Dam." That instantly became our reference to Windigo. Stan was smoking constantly and he would inhale so deep, I swore he could blow smoke rings out of his ass. Between drags, Stan would extol the benefits of being a Finn: "You know boys, if you blindfold a Finn, and spin him around and around, when he stops spinning, he will be pointing Nort!"

John Haapala, commercial fisherman, boat pilot, barber, and all around handyman was painting yet another one of the wooden scows that the Concession rented out to tourists. Why there weren't more deaths using those boats is beyond me. The Concession put a five and a half horse motor on a fourteen foot wood boat that weighed so much, I was amazed they floated. There was at least thirty pounds of paint on them, they all leaked, and sported about six inches of freeboard.

Haapala, it was rumored, only had one set of clothes for the entire summer. It was either that or he had several identical sets of shirts and pants. No one knew how old he was, but my Dad said he was a speed cop on the mainland when my Dad was a boy. Haapala would take two hundred forty-five steps to go fifty feet. He was about a half step faster than a statue. His neck appeared to be fused to his spine and if he had to turn to talk to you, he had to rotate his entire body. He chewed snuff constantly and had a Mona Lisa smile pasted on his face which caused a small amount of brown snuff juice to appear on the corners of his mouth. Nobody sat next to him at meal time.

My roommate and friend Bill Koskela was also a member of the advance party. I wasn't sure why, since he managed to escape the boat painting party and any other manual effort to prepare for the tourist invasion.

Sam introduced me to the garbage incinerator operator and suddenly, I was thankful to have Oarlocks as a roomie and not Cabbage, the incinerator operator. Cabbage (no one knew his real name), so named for the shape of his head, reveled in wading through the garbage and tossing it into the garbage crematorium. Cabbage was not only dumb, but disgusting, and smelled like a sack full of assholes. He would clear out the employee dining room when he arrived. He also had a partial set of teeth that would allow him to eat corn on the cob through a chain link fence.

We stopped by the maintenance shack and Wilho was splitting wood from the winter windfalls like a machine. He had a pile of wood that was approaching three cords. Digger was trying to make light conversation and said to Wilho, "Nice axe you got there, Wilho."

Wilho answered while never missing a beat, "It's been a good one too, and all it ever needed was three new handles and two new heads."

All of the locals that worked on the Island prior to us warned us never to get Wilho upset. Although they never saw him mad, they all were in awe of how strong he was. There was the story about an un-openable jar that all the guys took a shot at. Everyone waited for Wilho to come in for supper to see if he could get the lid to turn. Wilho put the death grip on the jar and started to turn the lid when the jar exploded in his hand. He picked the glass out of his hand, shrugged and proceeded to get in the chow line. I did notice his hands were incredibly big for a guy his size and his fingers looked like a bunch of bananas. When Wilho tested light sockets to see if they were "live," he just stuck a finger in it and he knew right away.

We left on June sixth because the Park Service boat bringing the NPC employees was due on June seventh. We were also scheduled to be on that boat. Digger and I reasoned, by virtue of our crossing, we would have a leg up impressing the female employees that signed on for the summer.

We went to bed with eager anticipation of meeting the *Ranger III* for the first time and meeting all of the NPC employees. Although I did know Bill from the mainland, I never slept in the same room as him. I didn't realize he snored like an eighteen wheeler downshifting and hitting the air brakes at the same time: "brraaaappppaaarrappp, schoooooschooooo."

We woke up to a beautiful day and we were jacked up with excitement waiting for the employee boat with its waitresses, hostesses, housekeepers, snack bar/gift shop clerks, and activity director. The NPC crew was made up of locals and imports recruited at the Mammoth Cave headquarters. Even though the headquarter boys were Bible thumpers, they always had a decent eye for pulchritude.

The sun was as brilliant as you will ever see it. Its light doesn't diminish as it passes through the Island's atmosphere. There is zero pollution and pollen. The deep blue water colliding with small rock cliffs, adorned with the deep green fir trees, and duplicated on hundreds of outer islands made me think that the easiest job on earth would be taking picture postcards on the Island. All you would have to do is load up the camera and start shooting from the hip.

Geologists tell us that over a billion years ago, a mantle plume of hot lava began working upward through the crust of what is known as the Canadian Shield. As the crust was thinned by the molten lava, it was also pulled apart, creating a rift which allowed for violent eruptions. The eruptions lasted for millions of years and began depressing the rift in the crust. The center of the rift is located in the middle of what became Lake Superior and the upward thrust of rock became Isle Royale.

This explains why there are gentle slopes in the Keweenaw Peninsula facing Isle Royale and gentle slopes on Isle Royale facing the Keweenaw Peninsula. On the opposite side of Isle Royale and the Keweenaw, there are sheer cliffs that drop straight into the water. One geologist explained it best: Take a ream of typing paper and hold it by the edges and the center will dip down representing the lake bed. As each side rises above the water, the land will slope up to the edge of the paper. The outside edges of the ream drop straight down, the same as the outside edges of the Keweenaw and Isle Royale.

After the eruptions, warm fluids continued to percolate through the fissures. The sediments picked up copper and iron ions which created the copper and iron ore deposits found in abundance in the U.P. The glaciers moved north and finished the job of filling the Great Lakes with water and making some landscaping changes.

A little know fact: Isle Royale is the third largest island in the forty eight contiguous United States, behind Long Island, New York and Padre Island, Texas.

The only downside to our plan of getting to the Island early was that the boys riding the boat had a seven hour head start in wooing the girls. If you do not stake out some ground in the first few days, it could prove to be a long, lonely summer. Isle Royale can quickly turn from the emerald jewel described in the poem "Hiawatha" to a summer sentence on Alcatraz.

We hoped our crossing would give us a little celebrity status even with the people that were seeing Lake Superior for the first time. The *Ranger III* takes about seven hours to cross from Houghton to the Island and the vastness of the Big Lake hits you when you get out in the middle and can't see land.

We had a game plan for the arriving employees. First, we would set an award winning fire in the Guest House Fireplace which was built in the day when that was the only heat in the building. The Guest House Fireplace (that is a proper name) could cruise at one and a half cords an hour, which required constant feeding, or you could engage the governor, and cut the consumption to about a half cord an hour!

Second, we would have some vodka, wine, and beer stashed nearby. This would, hopefully, put us into the elite status we would need to sift through the talent.

We were strolling on the dock, waiting for the *Ranger III,* and saw a school of herring in the small inner harbor surrounded by the Lodge, Dining Hall, and finger docks. Everyone was fascinated by the sheer number of fish. Digger and I grabbed our poles from the *Sisu* and rigged them with small gold gang hooks. The shiny hooks attracted the herring and by jerking the rod, you could snag one or two herring on almost every cast.

Dudley roared out of the Ranger shack and made a beeline toward us. He started screaming at us to stop the snagging instantly. He demanded we hand over our fishing rods and said he would take them and the fish. I knew snagging herring was perfectly legal, but I couldn't dissuade Dudley. Not only did he confiscate our equipment, but he was also going to issue tickets. As Dudley stormed back to the Ranger shack with our fishing rods and fish in tow, I began looking for Jim.

I tracked Jim down at his Park Service supplied house. Jim knew I was hopping mad. "That sonofabitch did it this time." I said, trying to keep my voice down.

"What sonofabitch, and what did he do?" Jim asked.

"Dudley, I mean Bob Davies. He took our fishing rods and threatened to fine us up the ass."

Jim was engaged now. "What the hell did you do?"

"We were snagging herring in the Inner Harbor and Dudley flew out of the Ranger shack, grabbed our rods, and started bellowing like a bull moose."

"Well, snagging is illegal," offered Jim.

"Not herring," I rebutted.

Jim grabbed his Smokey hat and said, "Let's go."

We hustled to the dock where Digger and Dudley were still jawing about the legality of snagging herring.

Dudley saw Jim and was still hopping up and down. "These idiots were snagging these fish right in front of us."

Jim said, "Let's call the Conservation Department and get a ruling."

This proved to be a time consuming task. Jim had to radio to the mainland and then they had to patch him into the local Conservation Office. Finally, the guy in charge got on the line and said that indeed, we were right.

Dudley was not remorseful. He said, "You Yooper Bundts may have won this battle, but I will win the war."

At this point, I was approaching Dudley with the worst of intents, and Jim jumped in between us. "This isn't a good way to begin the summer, boys."

At this point, I knew Jim was right and backed down. I couldn't resist a parting shot, "Bob, in a battle of wits, you are an unarmed man."

We put our rods away and went over the ridge to drink a couple of beers and cool our heels until the Employee boat was due.

We watched with eager anticipation as the Emps filed off the *Ranger III.* My eye caught an auburn haired beauty with a body to match. I found out her name was Kathy Hunter and I immediately invited her to the Guest House meet and greet that night.

Since I was a bell hop, one of my first jobs was to off-load the supplies on the *Ranger III.* The Captain, Woody, was one of my best friend's father. After greeting Woody, he gave me hell for crossing in a row boat, relayed more hell from my parents, and said we were damn lucky to make it. Woody went on to say that had the temperature not warmed up, we would have been totally socked in and likely to be still wandering around in open water.

I was very interested in the supply shipment as our counterpart on the mainland was to have loaded an egg carton with four cases of beer and a layer of eggs on top. Lurch was ready to face his first test of Herculean strength.

Since Lurch helped load the egg crate, he made sure no one else got near it. We piled all the supplies on the trailer which was pulled by a small Ford tractor (the only vehicle on the Island), and made sure we put the "eggs" on last.

Sam was watching the entire loading process and Lurch carried the "eggs" without breaking a sweat. Our first stop was the kitchen behind the dining room and we had a place all prepared to stash the beer shipment until dark.

Everything worked to perfection and we had an employee dinner in the regular dining room for the first and only time. We didn't know it then, but it was also the best meal we were going to have that summer. We cleared the meet and greet with Sam who made the announcement at dinner. Everyone was invited to get together at the Guest House lounge around eight in the evening.

The weather report for June seventh predicted the temperature would be in the low forties that night and as soon as we finished dinner, I went to the Guest House to prepare the fire. I never failed to be amazed at the size of that wood eater. If it wasn't for the fire, you could park a Buick four holer in that fireplace.

The Employees started coming in at the appointed time, and we had some Kingston Trio music playing on the stereo. The fire was perfect as Kathy walked through the door and my reaction was a barely audible "Holy moly!" Move over Natalie Wood! I could only wonder how someone that beautiful could have ended up on the Island!

Sam supplied some refreshments and snacks and everything was going according to plan. I asked Kathy if she wanted to "spruce up" her lemonade with a shot of Vodka. She just smiled and handed me the glass. I slipped outside to the stash and dumped in a couple of shots to cut down on the trips outside.

My roommate Bill Koskela was there and he was warming up the crowd, especially the girls, with some sea captain stories. Bill had an endearing quality about him that allowed him to get away with saying things that would ordinarily send a female employee running to the boss demanding a firing. For instance, if you asked him "How's it going, Bill?" then he would break out in his patented grin and reply, "Well youngster, any time you have the price of a beer and can still get a woody, how bad can it be?"

Bill was portly to be kind and I asked him if we should cool some beer for him. He said he would dearly love one, but as he put it, "I got my share and most of someone else's already." He had steely blue eyes that sometimes looked sad to me. If he was sad, he never showed it. To say he was unconventional was an understatement. He outfitted his fairly new Lincoln Continental with a working snow plow.

Bill had a captive audience and decided to give everyone the benefit of his vast experience. He said he had a cautionary tale regarding boats, and everyone should take heed, especially the boys. Considering this was an island and everyone would be in a boat at one time or another, everyone was listening.

"I was 'bout nineteen or twenty, and I took Elsie for da moonlit boat ride on Lake Medora," Bill remembered with his eyes cast heavenward, as if he was on Lake Medora that very evening.

"We rowed out to the middle of the lake, and I started to make my best moves," Bill recounted. We could only imagine.

"Effery-ding was perfect," Bill continued. "I even had some moonshine mixed wit lemonade, to sorta get Elsie in da mood."

"Well, boys and girls, the moonshine took aholt, and before a kot-dam mosquito could bite my ass, Elsie and me were tussling on da bottom of da boat," Bill relished.

"You shouda seen dat boat rock," Bill gaffed.

"Just about the time I was ready to go like tar paper, my balls got caught in da kot-dam oarlocks," Bill winced painfully.

"You coulda hit my pecker with a ball-peen hammer and it woodna hurt like dat," Bill whimpered.

"My balls hurt so hard, my brain stopped working, and I jumped up in dat kot-dam boat," Bill declared. His voice was showing an intensity that convinced us all.

"Looka dis; here I am standing up in da kot-dam boat with a kot-dam oar dangling from my balls," Bill wailed. He stood up to illustrate his predicament.

"Next ting I know, out da boat I go, wit dat kot-dam oar still hooked on my balls," Bill hollered.

"Well, Elsie yumped in da lake to save me, and lucky for me she's kot big floaters to hang on to," Bill smiled.

"We finally got da kot-dam oarlock unhooked from my balls and get in da boat," Bill recalls.

"So, my kawshun to you boys, is, watch out for dose kot-dam oarlocks," Bill counseled.

What would you call him? From that day til this one, Bill was "Oarlocks."

After Oarlocks' dissertation on the avoidance of oarlocks, I suggested to Kathy that we might take a moonlit boat ride. She looked duly impressed, as she asked, "Do you have a boat?"

I said "Not in Tobin Harbor, but I know where I can steal one."

The Smokeys had invited themselves to the get together and Dudley was all eyes as Kathy and I slipped out the back door.

There were a couple of NPC scows tied up in Tobin Harbor for housekeeping guests. The housekeeping cabins faced Tobin Harbor which was a two minute hike over the ridge, and a five mile ride (two and a half each way) by boat around Scoville Point.

Tobin Harbor was much quieter than Rock Harbor as there were no passenger boats and very few private boats tied up there. I headed for Scoville Point where there was a small bay and beach covered with Isle Royale sand. The grains of Isle Royale sand are about one to two inches in diameter. I figured that in another ten to twenty thousand years it will be a perfect sand beach.

Scoville Point was the perfect spot for sunsets, midnight campfires, cookouts, and beer parties. It even supplied us with a big rock in the cove where we could hide our boat in the unlikely event a Smokey wandered by at night.

I beached the boat and made a fire. All you need for a fire is some paper, as the beach is littered with driftwood from the

Canadian pulp mills. Earlier, I stashed a couple of six packs in the boat hoping Kathy would accept my invitation.

The northern lights were providing a show and we stayed there talking, drinking, and watching the light show until the wee hours. There was no moon so the stars and northern lights were in command of the skies. The northern lights were particularly active on this night, as if on cue. They were changing color from green to red and dancing like the horizon was on fire. When the northern lights took a break, the stars were so thick that they looked like sequins on a velvet curtain. Throw in some serious making out with a gorgeous woman and you have a top ten lifetime memory - maybe a top two or three. Suffer me.

Kathy was not only beautiful, but she had all the optional equipment. When Digger first saw her, he couldn't help employ the old saw, "You could play with those all night and never touch the same spot twice!" This led Digger to begin wondering how T&A material was allotted to a female at birth. Was there a T&A allotment board? Someone(s) must decide who gets what. My hair was starting to hurt.

Kathy just graduated from college and decided to see as much of the country as she could before settling down. She did some research and contacted the NPC boys in Mammoth Cave and they hired her for the Island. Thank you, boys!

Kathy grew up in Kansas where her Dad was a doctor and pillar of the community. What the hell was she doing going out with me? We were talking about what we wanted to do in the short term and she said she was hoping to spend the winter in Vail, skiing. Since I could skate better than I could walk, I thought, "I can ski."

The time flew by and it was time to leave if we hoped to get much more than a nap. We started picking our way in the darkness back toward the boat on the huge lava rock outcroppings that are everywhere on the Island. The next event conjured up a line from the poem *The Cremation of Sam McGee*; "The northern lights have seen queer sights, but queerest they ever did see." I was holding Kathy's hand and suddenly she disappeared into a narrow crevasse!

I tipped the scales at about 150 pounds with heavy shoes and Kathy was probably no more than 20 pounds lighter. At the instant she dropped into the crevasse, time almost stood still. I remember slipping my hand from hers and grabbing her wrist as I bent down. I never once thought that she would pull me down with her.

Not only did I stop her fall, but I pulled her back up to the top of the rock I was standing on in one motion.

We backed up a few feet and sat down. Kathy said, "How in the hell did you do that?" I told her I had no idea. I did remember reading about people that suddenly acquired inhuman strength during a moment of crisis. One account told the story of a father whose daughter was pinned beneath the gas tank of a car. Without thinking, he ran up and lifted the back of the car while others pulled his daughter to safety. The explanation was an extreme and instantaneous adrenaline rush.

I guess this was my herculean moment. We crawled to the edge of the crevasse; from what we could see, it appeared to be twenty feet deep and very narrow at the bottom. There was no way Kathy would not have suffered some severe injuries if she had fallen to the bottom. Not to mention the fact that I had no way to get her out without help.

I felt no ill effects from lifting at least 130 pounds with one hand while maintaining my balance on the edge of a precipice. I told Kathy, "If I could have someone scare the crap out of me, I could probably win the Olympic gold medal in weightlifting!"

The rest of our trip home was uneventful. Based on a "thank

you/romantic" kiss, I believed this was the moment that would keep us together for the summer. At least that was what I was thinking and I couldn't help hoping Kathy was thinking the same thing.

It was about three AM when I got back to my room and Oarlocks had his chain saw running full throttle. This is one case where a man lived up to his reputation. The sheer volume of his snoring was definitely measurable on a decibel meter. How he never woke himself up, I never knew.

Chapter 3

ISLAND LIFE

I was still dreaming about Kathy and our moonlight ride when the reality of my job was upon me. Lurch and I had to meet the Grumman *Goose* at ten in the morning, the Beech floatplane at eleven, and the *Isle Royale Queen II* at three thirty in the afternoon. The *Queen II* had a full boat according to their advanced radio transmissions to the office at Rock Harbor.

Unless you had a boat or good hiking shoes, your world was the area immediately around the Lodge. The Lodge is located at the northeast end of Rock Harbor in a little cove named Snug Harbor. Snug Harbor held the National Park Service Smokey station, general store, Smokey dorm, Post Office, gas pumps, dining room, and lodge rooms.

Snug Harbor also had a huge dock that could accommodate ocean going ships and was where the *Ranger III* and *Queen II* tied up. Toward the Lodge from the *Ranger III* dock there were five finger docks that were used for the National Park Concession scows or private boats. There was a large wooden dock straight out from the dining room, which was used by the *Voyageur,* and a large wooden dock at the tip of Snug Harbor that was the old *Ranger II* dock.

Rock Harbor is a deep water channel about eight miles long and is totally protected from the Big Lake by a string of many small islands that are almost connected. Isle Royale is surrounded by an archipelago of hundreds of outer islands. Rock Harbor was accessible through Smithwick Channel, a narrow opening straight out from the *Ranger III* dock, a wide channel from the northeast and a third opening six miles to the southwest, next to the NPS headquarters on Mott Island. The *Ranger III* used the Mott Island entrance and stopped at Mott to unload all of the NPS cargo and personnel.

The temperature on the Island rarely hits seventy degrees and campers are always surprised when their dishwater had a thin sheet of ice in the morning. The average high for June, July and August is sixty-six degrees. The average low for the same three months is forty-nine. It has snowed in all twelve months; however it was not measureable in June, July or August.

It was always amazing to greet the tourists seeing the Island for the first time. Some thought they were going to a luxurious resort island with five star amenities. They were the most disappointed. Some could adjust and some went back on the next boat or plane. During a previous summer, tourists were called Toads. The name stuck, so Toads they are.

Right after lunch, Lurch and I were hauling some new beds to the Lodge rooms. As we walked along the finger docks, we heard a war whoop coming across Snug Harbor from the old *Ranger II* dock. Scott and Mary Lou came running from the bushes, laughing and hollering as they crossed the dock bare ass naked and jumped into the lake. I knew Scott from back home and sold him a couple of six packs the night before. He swore he would be careful. I was glad he didn't get really reckless.

Lurch and I were two of a gang of people that witnessed this event. The most important witness was Sam who was waiting for them after they dressed and walked the trail back to the Lodge. They both got a ticket on the next *Ranger III* going back to the mainland. Although Scott was pretty shit-faced, he told Sam he brought the beer to the Island himself.

That would be the last time I sold any alcohol to an Emp. Digger used the occasion to make an observation of another way women were different than men. "How come," Digger mused, "do women's nipples get bigger in cold water, and men's dilly whackers disappear?" I think it was a rhetorical question.

The *Goose* was due and I headed up the hill to Tobin Harbor. Both planes landed in Tobin Harbor as the boat traffic in Rock Harbor made it too dangerous to use as a landing area. The *Goose* left the mainland from the Houghton County Airport but had to use a mooring buoy on the Island because of the fixed wing floats. The Twin Beech had floats in place of wheels and could ease up to the Tobin Harbor dock.

The *Goose*'s mooring buoy was about 150 feet from shore and required us to come along side with a NPC scow to off-load passengers and baggage. The *Goose* had a very thin fuselage and if you didn't bring the boat in just right, you could punch a hole in the side. Lurch couldn't operate an outboard, so we agreed I would meet the *Goose* and Lurch would meet the Beech. The sight of the *Goose* coming in for a touch down on water was always a sight to behold. Ned could keep the *Goose* on plane until he got close to the buoy. The landings were so smooth that most times the passengers couldn't tell if they were on the water or still in the air.

The 1943 Grumman *Goose* belonged to Chalks Airways in Miami and was piloted by Ned Ames who flew the *Goose* in the James Bond 007 film "Thunderball." Ned also flew the *Goose* in several commercials, was a fighter pilot in the Korean War and an all around great guy. Some years later, I found Ned was awarded two Distinguished Flying Crosses and nine Air Medals. He was also one of the first pilots to carry a nuclear bomb in an F-84.

The Twin Beech flew from the National Park Service mainland headquarters in Houghton, Michigan, which also was home base to the *Ranger III*.

Our best tips came from the plane people as they generally had more money than the boat people. We walked the tourists up a steep narrow trail from the Tobin Harbor dock about a half mile to the office to register. As soon as they registered, we took them to their rooms and went back for their luggage.

I made my first booze sale to a passenger on that first *Goose* run. Sure as hell, the first question they asked was, "Sonny, where can a person get a drink around here?"

My answer was a woeful, "Well sir, this is a dry island." After a pause, which I'm sure seemed like an eternity to the Toad, I added, "But there is a guy I know who might be able to get you a bottle of something."

Based on their facial expression and whether or not they licked their lips in anticipation, I knew how much the traffic would bear. "Well, sonny, I could sure use a bottle of Canadian whiskey," was the reply more often than not. I stocked Canadian whiskey, vodka, wine, and an ample supply of beer.

"I will check with the guy, and get back to you ASAP. By the way, he is a mercenary son of a bitch, and I know he ain't cheap." I tried to set the expectation level for the exorbitant prices I charged.

After waiting behind a tree, or taking more people to their rooms, resulting in more alcohol orders, I began with the first person that requested the libation. "He said he has a bottle left, but he wants twenty five dollars (retail cost was five dollars) for it. I told you he was an Ali Baba reincarnate." I consoled the shocked tourist.

The tourist almost never refused. He did bitch a bit. "That is outrageous, but I'll take it," was the usual reply.

Showing my compassionate side, I'd say, "I'll throw in a mixer and some ice if you wish."

This was the first *Ranger III* day with tourists and the dock was filled with people. There were Emps who had the day off, Smokeys, Lifers, and Tobanites. Lifers were people who still had life leases on their family cottages. Tobanites were Lifers from Tobin Harbor. Life leases weren't always the rule on the Island.

When the Department of Interior took over Isle Royale in 1946, they did not start off very well. The early bureaucrats felt they had a mandate to confiscate any and all properties using any means they felt necessary. In some cases, they burned the homes of fishermen with all of the contents inside. In one case, they burned a fisherman's house while he and his family watched. These heavy handed tactics and the lack of interest in the Island's history and its people caused some very tense moments between the Park Service and the residents. There is still some resentment to this day.

The inhabitants weren't your ordinary summer vacationers as the Island was accessible only in the summer and even then not so easily. It was hard to provision and had no electricity. To capture the essence of these early Islanders in a paragraph or a chapter isn't possible. Even an entire book would be tough. Their stories were all as unique as the Island they lived on. They were and still are some tough "Kot-damn Independents."

We can only guess that someone with juice got to the Feds in Washington and the practice of life leases was born. Each family could select one member (usually the youngest one) to be the life lease holder. Once that person died, the property would revert to the National Park. The NPS has made some changes to that policy by creating Special Use Permits that allows families to stay in their homes after the original lease holder dies.

Tobin Harbor still had about a dozen life lease holders and most of them were on hand to meet the *Ranger III*. The Tobanites lived in Tobin Harbor because of the natural shelter the harbor provided. Many lived on their own private island.

The Tobanites developed their own subculture and even had a newspaper called "The Tobin Talky."

If there was a Mayor of Tobin Harbor, it would be one the most famous Tobanites, Glen Merritt. He was always present when the *Ranger III* arrived, wearing Bermuda shorts, a short sleeved tropical shirt, and a bird nest hat. As the *Ranger III* docked, he would bellow out his traditional "whoop, whoop, whoop". I am sure some of the "first time" tourists wondered what they had signed on for.

Glen had just retired from his Postmaster's job in Duluth, Minnesota. He was a respected leader in Duluth, but he had a much more compelling family story. Glen's father was one of seven brothers that discovered the Mesabi Iron Range which was the richest iron ore find on the planet. The iron ore from the Mesabi Range is credited with being a major factor in our winning two world wars and making the United States a major world power.

The Merritt's did not share in the profits from their find, however, as the brothers had to move the iron ore from the Mesabi Range to Duluth for shipment to the steel factories in Pittsburgh and other industrial areas. Rockefeller loaned the boys money in return for Merritt stock and holdings as collateral and eventually, through legal maneuverings, cut the boys out entirely.

The Mesabi Range was one factor that helped Rockefeller upgrade from a millionaire to a billionaire. I don't think I could have been as calm as Glen was when he retold the story. In fact, I would have needed a straight jacket and spit bucket so as not to hurt myself or an innocent bystander.

When the *Ranger III* docked, we did everything from handling the ropes to taking the tourists to their rooms, to unloading the luggage and supplies. On the way to the kitchen to deliver the supplies, we stopped behind an abandoned Smokey shack and stashed the beer beneath the back porch.

We started running tourists to their rooms and I sold three six packs and two more bottles of liquor. Lurch wasn't as comfortable selling the booze as I was. Just as well, since business was good enough and I didn't want to call too much attention to myself.

I brought a single guy who walked with a limp to his room. I showed him how to control the drapes and turn on the heat (there was no need for air conditioning), and then I turned around to see the guy taking his pants off.

He said, "Can you give me a hand here?"

I was almost afraid to look, but as I turned around, he was talking about his artificial leg.

He continued, "This thing is killing me, and it is tough to take off."

At least he tipped well.

It was a busy initiation and I was roaming around the docks in Snug Harbor when the Captain of the *Ranger III,* Woody, walked over. His son Donny was one of my best friends and a key beer supplier. Donny worked for a construction company at Mott Island and he was supposed to bring me eight cases of beer from Mott that night.

Tuesday's *Ranger III* was the official "beer boat" for all of the Smokeys and construction guys on Mott Island. There was no beer on the *Ranger III* by the time it got to the Lodge.

Woody had some family information he wanted to relay to his son. Donny's twelve foot cedar boat was barely visible, but I could see that it was weaving down Rock Harbor. I figured it would be best if I could get Woody off the dock before Donny made his entrance. He was about an hour late, and the fact that he was running a slalom course could only mean he had been "pounding some Buds."

I offered to buy Woody a coffee while we waited for Donny, but Woody's years at sea gave him that sailor's long range vision. Woody said, "I think that is Don's boat coming down the harbor. See there, just past Tookers."

There was no dissuading Woody, so we just waited. The closer Don got, the drunker I knew he was. As they approached the finger docks, Donny's passenger, a Mott Island Sauce Dog, was standing near the bow of the boat with rope in hand, ready to tie up. I can still see Donny, hand on the tiller, classic shit-eating grin on his face, and throttling back way too late. Sauce Dog finally realized that they were not going to slow down enough for a normal docking and instant sobriety descended upon him.

It was a marvelous collision as the Sauce Dog catapulted out of the boat and went by Woody and me at an altitude of three feet. He actually cleared a six foot wide sidewalk and plowed about eight feet of gravel before coming to a stop. This was yet another definition of coming to the end of your rope.

Woody looked toward Scoville Point and in a voice that was barely audible, muttered, "Keeeeriest." He just turned and walked away. Donny was piss-your-pants laughing and I was becoming oxygen deprived. The madder Sauce Dog got, the more we laughed. I still do.

Donny had the foresight to disguise the beer under a bunch of life jackets and after Woody walked away, I took the boat a few hundred feet up Rock Harbor where Digger was waiting to off-load the booty.

As soon as the beer was stashed, I went to the Guest House to prepare for the evening's festivities. I had promised to start the evening fire and had a formal "date" with Kathy. I am not sure "date" is the correct word for taking someone, somewhere on the Island.

I got the fire started, and Digger supplied the music and the Emps started filing in. We were surprised to see Ellen Peters join the party. Ellen was the housekeeping supervisor and the self appointed dorm mother of the Emp dorm as well as chaperone and surrogate mother to all. Normally, she was drunk or passed out by this time, but not tonight. I think she was trying to make amends for her lunatic behavior a few nights before.

You couldn't tell how old Ellen was, but she took this job after her retirement. Even though she had a severe case of scoliosis, she could still move with the best of them. She would lead her crew to the rooms that needed cleaning and they all followed in what looked like a mini parade. The only difference was that the crew was all giving the finger to their parade leader. Ellen could never figure out what we were laughing at when we drove by on the luggage cart.

Ellen resembled the Hunchback of Notre Dame from a distance and was a dead ringer for the Wicked Witch of the West close-up.

Ellen had an amazing skill. She could keep an ash on her cigarette longer than the laws of physics should allow. Ellen would lean over the washing machine (actually, she was standing as straight as she could), and re-arrange the clothes with a two and a half inch ash hanging off the end of her butt. Everyone was silently rooting for the ash, but the ash never won. The second she moved back from the washer, the ash would hit the floor.

The Guest House lounge became the Emp's official meeting place because of an "Ellen incident" the week before. A bunch of us Emps were sitting in the lounge in the Emp dorm listening to records and telling tourist stories. At about ten that night, Ellen came storming down the stairs, butt dangling from her lips, screaming at the top of her lungs about the noise.

While she had her back turned, Digger yelled out a clever retort, "Go piss up a rope."

This really made her mad and she confronted everyone in the lounge, hoping for a Perry Mason confession. Everyone not being interrogated was snickering under their breaths as Ellen sped crablike over to the record player and pulled the needle across the entire record. The scratch didn't matter since she smashed whatever was playing at the time.

After Ellen retreated to her room, we agreed we would move the party to the Guest House from now on.

Digger knew I was going to go for a boat ride and asked to "double-date." He managed to get the Park Superintendant's daughter, Buffy, as his date. I was really skeptical about this one. Digger said he told her we had some refreshments left and were going to finish them off tonight.

We augmented our twenty-nine dollars per month salary with free food, free gas, and anything else they sold in the NPC General Store. Digger managed to appropriate a couple of steaks that we planned to cook on our private beach on Scoville Point. I ran the *Sisu* around to Tobin Harbor earlier and planned to take it on the cookout.

It was a perfect evening; the fire was going, the charcoal was getting grey, and we were having an aperitif or two. Buffy started getting a little squirrely after her first two beers, but we thought it was just some bureaucratese that had rubbed off on her, being the Super's daughter and all.

We cooked the steak, roasted a couple of potatoes and after dinner, partook of some after dinner drinks. We must have been preoccupied as we didn't notice the blanket of fog that rolled in. It reminded us of the crossing so we decided to forego Tobin Harbor. We opted for Rock Harbor because it was wider and easier to get home. Using the motor was too risky because we couldn't see a thing. By rowing, we could stay next to the shore and even though it was a two-and-half-mile row, it was safe.

We rowed for about fifteen minutes when Buffy decided to drop the motor and start it up. We were all hollering at her, but she wasn't going to be dissuaded. She said she knew where she was going and she had to get back. What do you do with a Park Superintendant's daughter who is that invincibly ignorant? Anyone else, we would have physically over-powered them.

Well, we drove around for what seemed like an eternity and I was praying we wouldn't hit the rocks or a reef. I was also praying that we weren't headed for open water. In reality we probably were going for less than ten minutes. Once again, my faith in a Supreme Force was renewed.

Buffy shut the motor off and announced to no one's surprise, "I don't know where we are." That made four of us.

Luckily, the fog horn on Passage Island some seven miles away was audible. Digger and I rowed perpendicular to the sound toward the Island and hoped we had not cleared the northern end which would have us rowing to Canada. After a half hour of rowing, we got back to what we hoped was the Island side of Rock Harbor and not the Island side of one of the outer islands.

We made a left turn and rowed for about an hour and finally made it back to Snug Harbor. Memo to the file: "Never double date with Buffy and anybody."

As we passed the Lodge units, we saw two of the housekeeping crew coming out of one of the rooms. One of the few benefits of working for Ellen was having a pass key to all rooms and knowing what rooms were empty. Nothing like a lake view room with the moon shimmering off of the water to get someone in the mood.

I had a pass key, but there was a night watchman that was a taller version of Lon Chaney. There was no doubt that even his daydreams were nightmares. I didn't think the risk was worth the reward, since a dalliance in a Lodge room was sure to merit a one way ticket home.

It was three AM, so about all I could do was give Kathy a good night kiss and head for the sound of the chainsaw.

We had another full day with the *Ranger III* leaving and the *Queen II* and *Voyageur* , along with two planes full, coming. I was busier than a one legged man at an ass kicking party unloading the *Queen II* and I ran past a woman sitting with two kids on one of the benches, crying. I stopped to find out what she was crying about and she said they had no Coleman fuel for their Coleman stove. They couldn't carry it on the boat and the store was sold out. She was sobbing and her two little boys were crying and the husband looked like he was on his way to the firing squad.

The wife said they had been planning and saving for this vacation for a year and now it was all ruined. The husband introduced himself as Tom, his wife, Janice, and the two boys, Mike and Jim. Tom said he went to the Smokey station and they were unable to help him.

I was having a tough time watching them and blurted out, "Don't worry. I'll come up with something as soon as I get all these people to their rooms."

As we rode away, Lurch said, "Looks like you let your mouth overload your ass on this one."

Every time I passed them, they looked at me like their last hope on earth. I almost started crying. I started imaging all sorts of things like their anticipation of their "once in a lifetime vacation and now this."

I had no idea how I was going to produce Coleman fuel for this family, and since they weren't staying at the Lodge, it wasn't my responsibility anyway. I passed Wilho on one of our trips to the *Ranger III* and asked him if they had any Coleman fuel in the maintenance shack. "Nope," replied Wilho. His total word count for the summer ballooned to forty seven with this answer.

Then I recalled that there was an old oil drum in one of the storage shacks. I ran to the shack and found the barrel half full and was labeled "White Naptha." Oarlocks was regaling a few tourists with the story about how all the outer islands were placed there by the Park Service and held there by underwater cables. I interrupted his naturalist seminar and asked him what White Naptha was.

Oarlocks said it was an old time way of labeling white gas, which was also the same as today's Coleman fuel. I ran to the bench where the Family Destitute was sitting and told them I may have a solution.

I don't think I would have gotten a better reaction if I told them I was Michael Anthony and they just won a million bucks.

I could feel sweat on my forehead. It may not have been such a good idea to declare victory before testing the white Naptha. The thought that maybe it wasn't white Naptha also crossed my mind. My next thought was, "That shit better work in a Coleman stove."

We got everyone settled in and I got a can and a hand pump and filled the can. At least the stuff looked like white gas. We poured it in the stove, pumped up the pressure, and lit a match. I was visibly sweating as Tom held the match to the burner and it sprang to life, sporting a beautiful blue flame.

Janice kissed me, Tom shook my hand, and the boys were hopping up and down. They did just win a million, or its equivalent, and I chalked it up to one more affirmation that there is a God.

They were willing to pay anything, but I told them to chalk it up to Isle Royale hospitality. Besides, their reaction was the best tip I got all summer.

Tom offered that someday I would probably own the Island. I told him, I already did and so did he.

The *Voyageur* was due in tonight and the crew consisted of two guys, Captain Roy and First Mate Merle. They sailed from Grand Portage, Minnesota and circumnavigated the Island three times a week. Theirs was the official US Mail boat and they also stopped at the various fishermen and families still left on the Island to drop off mail and supplies. Their exploits were legendary and their stories could easily fill a book.

On one of their earlier trips, they were hauling gas and passengers which is not allowed by Coast Guard rules. As the Coast Guard approached, Roy and Merle made all of the passengers into crew members.

This trip was a legitimate passenger trip and they always stopped in Tobin Harbor at the NPS dock to off-load mail and supplies for the Tobanites. The Tobanites were all waiting for the *Voyageur* and a professor from the University of Wisconsin had his 55 foot Chris Craft tied up in the only dock space that could accommodate the *Voyageur*.

One of the Tobanites politely informed the Professor that the *Voyageur* was due and this was the only place he could tie up. The Professor in turn pretty much told the Tobanites to shove it, as he was not moving and furthermore, the dock belonged to the National Park Service which gave him as much right to its use as the *Voyageur*. This is how the Professor earned his new moniker as Professor Asshole (PA).

PA was on a paid vacation from the University under the guise of conducting a wolf study. Actually, the Professor vacationed and drank on his boat on the taxpayer's dime while the study was conducted by his students. Naturally, PA took credit for the entire published information put out by his students and is still revered by the Audubon Society and the Sierra Club. I did hear that in times gone by, PA did some legitimate and good work studying wolves. It seemed he was not only resting on his laurels, but he was sitting in the fire with someone else's ass. While we were there, that ass belonged to a guy around our age that would become one of the planet's greatest authorities on wolves.

This was as close to a riot conducted by a group of senior citizens as you will ever see. The *Voyageur* arrived right on schedule and Roy pulled along side PA's boat and asked if he would cast off while they unloaded.

"I'm staying," replied PA.

Without hesitation or another word, Merle was tying up to PA's boat and before PA could muster a protest, Merle threw the mail bag onto the teak deck and started off-loading supplies.

With that, a couple of the younger Tobanites jumped on board and began carrying the supplies across PA's deck. Roy was working the engine to keep both the *Voyageur* and PA's boat pressed against the dock.

Needless to say, it was the last time PA tied up at that dock when the *Voyageur* was due.

Roy and Merle had a finely tuned act when they steamed into Snug Harbor to tie up at the *Voyageur* dock. Roy came in hot and Merle would stand up on the stern, rope in hand, looking straight ahead. Roy would throw it in reverse and just as the boat stopped, Merle would step off without looking, bend down, and put a few wraps around the cleat still staring straight ahead. This always got a standing ovation from the passengers and the people on the dock.

They were great guys, but they would unload the luggage without any tags. It took us a long time to match the luggage with the people. I told the boys that if they would tag the bags, I would supply the tags and throw in a coffee and pie at the snack bar.

Next trip, sure enough, there were tags on every bag. I told Roy and Merle their coffee and pie were waiting as I started taking the passengers to their rooms. When we had everyone in their rooms, Lurch and I went back for the luggage.

Every bag was tagged all right. Two bags were labeled "2W." Another one was tagged "SM." There were three more with "MWB."

I went to the snack bar where the boys were eating their pie and grinning. "How are the tags working out?" Merle inquired.

"I am just a little confused Merle," I confessed. "What the hell is "2W," "SM," "MWB?"

Merle looked at me with a "How stupid can you be?" look. "It's simple," Merle counseled. "2W are those two women that were together, SM was that Single Man, and MWB belongs to the man, woman and boy."

"Enjoy the pie, boys," was about all I could muster as I left.

John Haapala was our unofficial barber. It wasn't like he needed the money as I am sure John had the first buck he ever made. I mentioned the fact that his body was one immovable piece and the perpetual chew of Copenhagen snuff hid behind his bottom lip accounted for his Mona Lisa smile and the brown juice on the corners of his mouth.

The "shop" was next to the employee's dorm where there was an outlet for his clippers and a Westinghouse AM radio that looked like a loaf of bread standing on end. John listened to a barely audible station from Canada, presumably, so he would know if we were at war or some other equally important event.

The "shop" was open on Wednesday night from six to eight. It would take him thirty minutes to set up the shop which included a stool, bed sheet, instruments, and granny glasses.

He was only open if it didn't rain, and you had to make an appointment even though John had nothing to do and nowhere to go. Certain people (I was one) could get a haircut by special request, but you had to know John considered you privileged and you had to let John know you knew.

A haircut cost fifty cents and the tip was another fifty cents. Find another barber if you didn't tip, because John was always too busy for non-tippers. You also had to endure a liberal dose of barnyard philosophy.

John was very suspicious of our space program. He was convinced that all of the space shots were an elaborate ruse produced in a Hollywood studio. When John found out we were going to go to the moon, he would tell you, "The kot-tam moon is three, maybe four hunnert miles away. Hell, dats like going from Hancock to da Mackinaw Bridge straight up in da air! No kot-tam vay!"

One of John's favorite hobbies was giving the Toads misinformation. We played into this until it began to negatively impact on our tips.

After a rough crossing, there were always plenty of walking wounded. You didn't have to be a Mensa member to pick out the sick Toads. There is nothing attractive about a person who has spent the past four hours projectile vomiting over the rail of a pitching boat. Usually, their complexion was green, their eyes glassed over, and their hair looked like it had been combed with firecrackers. If you have ever been seasick you know; first you're afraid you'll die, and then you're afraid you won't.

I was practically carrying this little old, very green lady. The green is the result of throwing up liver bile. I figured she had a few bucks as she was dressed in a mink coat. She whispered as best as she could, "Sonny is there seaplane service from this Island?" I assured her there was. "Good," her eyes brightened a bit, "that will save me from buying one."

I booked her on the *Goose* for her return trip.

There were always a few that wanted to know what could be done to combat this scourge. If John Haapala wasn't around, we prescribed Dramamine. If John was around, we would refer the tourist to him. "You see, John has spent most of his life on the Big Lake and no one has ever seen him sick," we would offer as proof.

The green Toads would seek John out and I am sure they

never felt humbler at any other time in their lives. "I understand you are a boat captain and know what can be done to combat sea sickness," the Toad would grovel.

"Well," John talked at the same speed he walked, "the only thing you can do is tie a chunk of bacon fat on a piece of string," he would begin. Green people aren't anxious to think about bacon fat tied to a piece of string. John would smile (only we could tell John was smiling) and continue, "then you run that bacon fat up and down your throat to grease the tube." This was the only time John would move his head independently of his body. He would tilt his head back to illustrate and move his arm up and down over his mouth. "That way, the big chunks don't hurt as much."

No matter how many times I heard the story, I couldn't help laughing like hell. John just stood there looking at the Toad as he/she turned one more shade of green and threw up again.

Jim Kangas came up to me and said he got a call from Park Headquarters. He said someone reported an open fire at Scoville Point. I said, "Let me guess who reported this serious violation; were his initials Dudley Dooright?"

"Good guess," Jim said. "But, I still have to ask if you know anything about that."

"As a matter of fact, I do know a few things about Scoville. There isn't anything but rocks for hundreds of feet and except for volcanoes; I have never heard of rocks catching fire. Second, I heard tell there was a guy named Beam out there. Jim Beam that is and he is on his way to visit you."

"I didn't think you were involved," Jim replied, "but I had to ask."

Digger and I had a meeting that night to step up the program on Dudley. He was really starting to be a royal pain. We decided that Dudley should find out what all-pro ball-busters could do.

A few Emps and a couple cooks approached me with a plea

to talk to John about his eating habits. John would sit in the dining room and roll his food around in is mouth like he was sorting out what he wanted to chew. This resulted in some very unappetizing moments as he couldn't do the sorting operation with his mouth closed. They knew I was as close to being a friend of John Haapala's as anyone could be, but I figured I had enough enemies. Besides, how do you stop a habit that had been going on for a lifetime?

In my book, this habit took a distant second to John's number one trait, farting. John would "let her rip" with any number of follow up comments like: "Catch that one and paint 'er green," "You coulda heated two houses for a winter with that one," or "That was a purple streamer."

Tony's title was that of Second Cook. No matter that all the cooks except for Eleana, the head cook, made little more than the minimum wage. They took their titles seriously. Because of that, Tony seldom spoke to the dishwashers except to bark out orders. He took delight in burning pots and pans just to watch the dishwashers scour them to his liking. The dishwashers gingerly mentioned this to Tony, but all it did was cause an increase in the number of burned pots.

Being the doers of getting things done, the dishwashers asked us what could be done. Simple, offered Digger. "Next time he burns one, it disappears. The woods behind the incinerator would be a good spot; no one ever goes up there." It only took two pots before Tony caught on, perhaps due to the fact that one of them was Tony's favorite. Burning was kept to a minimum and there was a cease-fire between the cooks and the dishwashers.

The dishwashers also had a problem with the attitude of one of the hostesses. We believed she really didn't want to be there, and treated everyone else as serfs. We believed she thought of herself as the "Royal Princess." Ms. Princess did come from several generations of Island lifers, so perhaps that is where her sense of entitlement came from. She was particularly tough on the dishwashers and they wondered if we had any suggestions to bring her closer to earth.

It took us a day, but we noticed that one of her few duties was to take the silverware from the towel after it was clean and either set a table or store it in the silverware tray. We suggested that the dishwashers wait until she really needed silverware and then take it from the one hundred eighty degree water and place it on the towel just before she re-entered the kitchen. As she grabbed the smoking hot silverware and screamed, the dishwashers replied in unison, "Hot eh?" When she complained that she should have been warned, the boys said she gave them the impression that she didn't want to be talked to by the peons. It thawed her a little, but she left halfway through the summer; presumably, back to the Kingdom.

Dudley and the other Smokeys decided they would throw a party for the NPC girls. Kathy asked if I minded if she went and I said "No problem-if we can't beat a Smokey in any game, we should go home." Another thought I had was that Dudley couldn't make out in a woman's prison with a handful of pardons.

Digger added, "Dudley couldn't make out in a whore house with a fistful of hundreds."

The Smokey house was one of the nicest Rock Harbor homes built by one of the original Island families. The house was on the side of the ridge toward Tobin Harbor.

The Smokeys built a beautiful fire in their living room fireplace, made some hors d'oeuvres, appropriated some beer, and were all set to cut us out of the female equation. We didn't think the Smokeys could ace us out, but we also didn't want to take any chances.

The Smokey house was built on a slope and there was easy

access to the roof. We soaked half of a large piece of cardboard with water and connected the dry half to a rope.

Just as the party started to heat up, we leaned a step ladder on the back of the Smokey den, climbed on the roof, and put the wet half of the cardboard over the chimney opening. I quickly got off the roof, grabbed the ladder and beat a hasty retreat up the ridge.

We had two hundred feet of rope, connected to our cardboard, courtesy of the Park Service. As soon as we heard the shuffling of many feet, we pulled the cardboard off the chimney up to our position on the ridge. The Smokeys and the girls ran out of the Smokey den like someone just unloaded a sack of snakes.

Digger returned to the maintenance shack with the step ladder and I coiled the rope and carried the cardboard high on the ridge. I hid the cardboard under a fir whose branches arched to the ground and brought the rope back to Digger's room.

We went to the Emp lounge and it wasn't long before the girls came in still rubbing their eyes and coughing. We asked what happened and they mumbled something about the stupid Smokeys who couldn't even build a fire. No sooner had the girls disappeared to get a shower when Dudley and a couple of his Smokey buddies burst through the door. Between coughs they started hollering at us.

Digger didn't help the situation when he calmly looked at Dudley and asked, "Where was the forest fire and were you able to put it out?"

It looked like there was smoke coming out of Dudley's ears, and we couldn't tell if it was from the fire or that his brain was overheating. Dudley proclaimed, "I don't know how you guys were involved, but I know you were. If it is the last thing I do, I will see that you both are banished from this Island."

The next day we placed a huge sign in Dudley's boat which read, "Remember: only YOU can prevent forest fires."

Mother Duck gave birth to a large brood in June. She was a mallard and she must have just gone through a divorce as we never saw the father. There were ten ducklings following Mommy around Snug Harbor. They swam around the docks and they never wanted for food. Mommy and the brood were the hit of the harbor, but not for long.

It didn't take long for the seagulls to find the brood. The ducklings wandered a little distance from the finger docks and the seagulls were on them. Mother Mallard tried her best to defend her brood, but the seagulls drove her away and got all but one duckling. We drove the seagulls away and the lone survivor beat it back to the safety of the finger docks.

The Mother Mallard was nowhere to be found and we figured she thought she lost her entire family. The lone survivor was so small we figured its chances of survival were about the same as a cellophane dog being able to catch an asbestos cat in hell.

Much to our surprise, the lone duckling was still swimming around the finger docks the next day. One of the girls named it Herman. Herman never had to wonder where his next meal was coming from and he never wandered far from the relative safety of the finger docks. We all took turns chasing the seagulls whenever they came looking for Herman. He was smart enough to duck under the docks or behind a boat whenever a seagull got close.

Herman became our official mascot and was a survivor par excellence. He would eat out of our hands and we could probably have picked him up.

This brings me to another instance where sand gets into the gears that turn my logical thoughts. One is allowed to shoot ducks, but seagulls that are nothing more than seagoing pigeons are protected by federal law. Suffer me.

Chapter 4

LET THE GAMES BEGIN

At first they were a mild annoyance. Now, the Smokeys were really beginning to affect our daily lives. A by-product of the Smokey interference was causing discord among our fellow Concession Emps.

Although Dudley was leading the charge to make our lives miserable, it almost didn't seem fair to run rough shod just over him, since it was pretty much man versus twit.

Dudley will go far in the Department of the Interior. He has all of the "right stuff"; he's dumb, a social misfit, a pathological ass kisser, and an enforcer of rules he doesn't understand. I am sure he never had an original thought.

Thomas Reed, the Speaker of the House of Representatives, in the 1800's said something one could apply to Dudley and some of his ilk: "They never opened their mouths without subtracting from the sum of human knowledge."

We made a mental list of the Smokeys that were in Dudley's camp. We figured even expanding our program to a few dozen Smokeys would still leave us with an overwhelming advantage.

Bob Koski sent us a shipment of M-80 fire crackers which

were the equivalent of an eighth stick of dynamite. We were going to use them for "fishing" in Duncan Harbor. Duncan

Harbor was home to a bunch of four foot northern pikes sunning themselves in the shallows and ignoring every lure we threw at them.

We figured we could sacrifice a couple of "fish lure" M-80's to give the Smokeys something to think about. It was a calm, moonless night and we decided to shake up the top brass at National Park Headquarters on Mott Island. Mott is a small outer Island some five miles from Snug Harbor and the Lodge. All of the activity and access to Mott was on the Rock Harbor side of the Island. There is no access directly from Mott to the Big Lake.

We took the *Sisu* outside of Rock Harbor until we got to the Big Lake side of Mott. We had a full five gallon gas can and poured all five gallons into the water. Then we lit a couple of M-80's and threw them into the gas slick.

Holy shit! Not only was the explosion ear deafening, but the gas ignited and the flames shot up fifteen to twenty feet. The flaming water started to surround our boat and it was lucky we didn't turn the motor off, as we just barely shot through the flames and started back to the Rock.

To the observers on Mott Island, it must have sounded like an explosion on a boat and the boat was now on fire.

I didn't know they had a siren on Mott, but I know now. It sounded like all hell was breaking loose as they mobilized the troops and we took off like an atheist from a revival meeting.

In order to get to the Big Lake side of Mott, the Smokeys would have to go west for a mile or so and then swing out into the open water and head east for a mile or so.

Luckily we were headed east and we were probably back at the Rock by the time they reached the explosion site. We decided not to enter Snug Harbor, but go around the point and dock over the ridge in Tobin Harbor.

We tied up and calmly walked into the employee dining room and poured a cup of coffee. We finished our coffee and walked out to the Lodge area. Jim was running from the Smokey shack and immediately sought us out. "Where were you guys tonight?" was Jim's first question.

I told him Kathy and I took a short stroll toward Scoville Point. Digger said he was in his room reading "Moldy Dick," a true story about Dudley. "Why do you ask?" Perhaps Digger smiled a little too much.

"Mott radioed and said there were a couple of explosions and a huge fire behind Mott," Jim answered. "By the time they got there, the fire was gone and there was no evidence of a boat. I don't suppose you know anything about that?"

"Well," Digger offered, "sounds like you got a disgruntled employee down there at Mott. Have you checked the whereabouts of Dudley?"

Jim said he was just responding to the request from Mott to check on our whereabouts and he would verify that we were both in the Harbor during the "event."

I could do most any job in our organization and on this day I was working three jobs to cover for some days off. Besides bell hopping, I was the dock attendant and garbage man. There was a short lull in the action, and I went into the coffee shop for a quick cup of Joe. I could have gone to the Emp dining room, but I had to keep an eye on the dock. As I was mixing cream and sugar in my cup, the waitress informed me that coffee was no longer free to Emps in the snack bar. She would put fifty cents on my bill if I wished. I said that would not be necessary, as I would return the coffee. I poured the mixed cup back into the pot and walked out.

Ten minutes later, Sam was heading my way like a guided missile. He was definitely perturbed and looked like he was getting madder with every step. When he finally got to me on the dock, he said Sally was crying in the snack bar because I ruined an entire pot of coffee.

I explained to the boss that I would have gone to the Emp dining room, but I had to keep an eye on the dock and I was working three jobs today. Besides, no one told us they were going to start charging for coffee in the snack bar. Sam was a reasonable man and thought for a minute and said he would consider amending the rules. He also said he was still going to charge me two dollars for ruining a pot of coffee.

I couldn't help mentioning that two plus days' pay seemed a little stiff of a punishment. Also, a half day's pay for a cup of Joe while working didn't square either.

Sam went back to free coffee in the snack bar for anyone working.

It turned out it wasn't our imagination that the Park Service was going after Digger and me. Jim Kangas verified that Digger and I were put on the NPS "watch list." Jim was the only Smokey I trusted and I slipped him a bottle of Jim Beam now and then to solidify our mutual trust.

Dudley must have gotten the word as well, and this only made him more aggressive in busting our balls. Dudley complained to Jim that a Smokey should be handling the ropes when the *Ranger III* came in, seeing as how it was a Park Service boat and all. Jim was almost apologetic when he told me Dudley wanted to catch the lead rope from the *Ranger III.* I assured Jim that it was not the highlight of my summer to catch the rope and that we welcomed Dudley's offer.

I had some time between boats and planes and decided to troll around Scoville point for an hour. Dudley must have been doing his homework and came running when he saw me untying the *Sisu*.

"Hold it," he bellowed. "Your boat is not compliant and you ain't going anywhere."

"Dudley, please lower your voice and speak in a low roar," I replied, knowing it would piss him off.

Dudley had some sort of official form filled out with all of the "violations" of the *Sisu*. I had no running lights, fire extinguisher, or the proper Coast Guard approved life preservers. Dudley also suggested that I get an anchor with the appropriate length of rope.

I reminded Dudley that most places around the Island were three hundred feet deep, two feet from shore.

"How many times have you used an anchor this summer?" I asked.

"That's irrelevant," Dudley snapped back.

I gave him that one. "Did you mention this to Jim?"

"Not only did I mention it to Jim, but he is on board with it."

"Well, I want to hear it from Jim personally," I shot back.

"That won't be necessary, but you have until Thursday to be compliant."

Jim must have told Dudley to give me a grace period to comply. He stomped off and shot over his shoulder, "You have until Thursday and after that, I will impound your tin tub until the end of the summer."

I bee-lasted to Scoville and dropped a trolling lure. I barely finished letting the line out when I got a strike. A beautiful five pound lake trout was in the boat and I still had most of an hour to fish. I caught four more on my lunch hour and headed back to the Lodge.

I returned to the Lodge and filleted the trout. I gave the filets to Eleana. She was expecting her son to visit and I knew she could do them justice.

Reality was upon me as the Toads were descending from everywhere. Lurch and I were a finely tuned act by now and the Toads were letting the Boss know how happy they were with our service.

As soon as we finished unloading the *Ranger III* that night, Digger and I took a trip to Park Headquarters on Mott Island where there was a world class repair shop for all of the Park Service boats and equipment. The shop was managed by a fellow Yooper and boat mechanic par excellence, Jack Jacobs.

We parked in an out-of-the-way dock and walked to the shop and found Jack. "Hi Jack. I've got a small problem I thought you might be able to help me with," I began. "One of the Smokey trainees at the Rock is busting my balls and he is going to take my boat if I don't make it Coast Guard compliant."

"What do you need?" Jack asked.

I went over the list with Jack and he suggested we get lost for an hour or so. Digger and I went to the Big Lake side of the Island and sat on the rocks for an hour. When we got back, the boat was tied up at the same dock, resplendent with running lights, fire extinguisher, and new life jackets. Jack said, "I threw in a tune-up to help off-set the hassle."

I handed Jack the bottle of Canadian Club I brought with me and we took off for the Rock. Whiskey worked better than money on the Island.

I kept the *Sisu* out of sight until the Thursday deadline and tied it up near the Smokey Station. Right on cue, Dudley came storming out of the office and made a beeline to the *Sisu*. Only opening my presents on Christmas morning gave me a bigger kick than seeing Dudley's jaw drop. "How in the hell did you do this?" an astounded Dudley asked.

I told him, "I had the stuff all along, but I just never had the time to install it."

Digger stated the obvious, "Enough was enough." This was war.

Dudley and the other trainees conducted a scripted Isle Royale lecture/slide show, five nights a week in the Recreation Hall. Dudley had Tuesdays and Thursdays.

We were trying to figure a way to disrupt Dudley's lecture and remain blameless. After a couple of Budweiser brainstorming sessions, we came up with the idea of playing with the lights. When the Smokeys started their slide show, they would turn off all the lights in order to better see the screen.

We intercepted the wire going to the inside light switch, and spliced a wire to it above the ceiling, then ran it out to the eave on the outside of the building. Next, we connected the wire to a switch and screwed it to a roof joist. We hooked two strings on the switch, pulling in opposite directions so we could toggle the switch back and forth. To hide the strings, we threaded them through eye hooks under the eaves so we could stand behind the building and still operate the switch. We could reverse the effects of the inside switch whenever we pulled one of the two strings. Just as the presentation got to an interesting part, I pulled one of the strings, and voila, lights on.

This would force Dudley to go to the back of the room and turn the lights off. Sometimes, I turned them off by pulling the other string before he got to the switch. Other times, I would turn them back on as soon as he got back to the lecture.

Once in a while, Digger or I would attend the lecture while the other operated the lights. Dudley was not very good at improv and he got all disoriented when we tripped the light-fantastic. There is no doubt we increased his anxiety level just by being present. When we finally let him continue, he stuttered and stammered, and once in a while, people in the audience walked out.

We never showed any emotion when Dudley melted down.

That might tip our hand. Digger actually consoled Dudley after a couple of debacles.

Dudley had the switch replaced and we kept it up for over a month. We were clearly driving him nuts. No other Smokey reported any problem with the lights.

All the outboards we ran were equipped with shear pins. Shear pins are a soft metal rod about two inches long and an eighth to a quarter inch in diameter. The pin would "shear" in half if your propeller hit hard water, such as a rock.

Shearing the shear pin was preferable to destroying the propeller, lower unit, or gear box. We became experts at replacing shear pins as we operated in shallow water a lot. All you had to do was remove the prop by straightening a cotter pin, unscrewing the prop, and pushing the "sheared" shear pin through with a new one.

We also were experts at sneaking down to Dudley's and the other Smokey boats late at night and shearing an otherwise good shear pin. It took a while for Dudley and the others to figure out how to repair a shear pin. Meanwhile, they never figured out how this was happening. Even their boss Jim was chewing them out for hitting "hard" water.

One morning, Jim got a distress call from a boat in trouble near the end of the Island. Dudley's boat was the only one available and Jim cast off only to find the shear pin had to be replaced. It took a little time to replace the pin and I told Jim to use the *Sisu*. It wasn't as fast as Dudley's boat, but it was still faster than replacing the shear pin.

About an hour later, Jim was towing a small boat into the Harbor with a couple of scared Toads. They were going to go around Blake Point and the waves were breaking over their bow. A passing ore boat saw them waving and radioed the Park Service. I guess their number wasn't pulled on this day.

That was the end of the broken shear pins.

Ned, the *Goose* pilot, shared our understanding of the Park Service, but had to be very careful to make his official position that of one hundred percent behind everything they did. Ned had to jump through hoops to get a permit to fly the *Goose* to the Island and he didn't want to do anything to jeopardize it.

Ned said some BI (Bureaucratic Idiot) in Washington told the BI Superintendant on the Island that he would have to store four hundred gallons of aviation gas on the Island. There didn't seem to be any rationale given to this requirement, it just was.

I believed this was an example of the Park Service's not so veiled favoritism of the Beech Boy.

Ned said the gas was due to get delivered via barge today and wondered if I could give him a hand to store them per BI instructions.

The aviation gas arrived in fifty five gallon drums and the tug pushing the barge set them on the dock next to the gas pumps. Each barrel weighed about four hundred pounds and the Park Service wanted them stored on the ridge in a barely accessible area.

We devised a ramp system to get them on the trailer so we could tow them with the Ford tractor. Lurch, Digger, and I cleared rocks and small trees to make a trail we could drive on to get the barrels to their final destination.

The trail was steep and the tractor was old, so we waited until the Boss wasn't around. I am not sure he would want to risk his only baggage/supply hauler humping barrels of gas up a rock strewn hill.

We decided that we would have to go it one barrel at a time due to the weight and steepness of the trail. After we loaded the barrel, we lashed it in and stationed Digger and Lurch in the trailer to further stabilize the cargo. The last thing you need is a barrel of one hundred octane aviation gas rolling down the hill toward the Lodge area.

We finished the job and Ned was grateful. He said we could ride the *Goose* anytime there was an open seat. When he asked if there was anything else he could do, I said, "Perhaps, but I will tell you later." I figured if I got really low on liquor reserves, Ned would bring me a bottle or three.

There were a couple of Smokeys besides Jim that we were friendly with. I even sold them some beer. They invited us up to the Smokey den a few times to return the favor. During one of those get-togethers I noticed a bottle of Head and Shoulders in the bathroom. This bathroom was shared by Dudley and another Smokey.

As a peace offering, we told the Smokeys we would provide the refreshments for a "bury the hatchet" meeting. They jumped at the idea of free beer, but I wasn't sure how much they were willing to forgive and forget.

A good time was being had by all and during one of Digger's trips to Dudley's bathroom; he replaced the Head and Shoulders shampoo with Nair. They both looked the same and had the same consistency. The difference is that Nair is a very effective hair remover.

The next day, Dudley had his hat pulled down extra tight and when we saw him at the Smokey station, we were thankful he wasn't allowed to carry a gun.

We asked Jim what was bothering Dudley and Jim said we really did it this time. He said Dudley "shampooed" his hair this morning and much to his horror, his hair was falling out in clumps. His roommate suggested that he wash it again, which he did, only to have more of it fall out.

Jim said it looked like someone spun Dudley around in a barber chair and whacked chunks out with a bull whip. Jim kinda chuckled, I swear.

Jim went on, "You boys are shit for the birds right now. There isn't anything I can do to protect you. You're on your own."

Just then, Dudley came storming down to the dock with smoke coming out of his ears. I figured we were going to go a couple of rounds at least. He came to a couple inches of Digger's face and said, "I will get you both off of this Island one way or another and you are damn lucky Jim is here."

About all the threat did was to let Digger dust off some of his one-liners that he had been dying to use: "Get your gang and tell the big ones to line up and the little ones to bunch up. You'd be further ahead jacking off a bobcat with a handful of cockleburrs."

Dudley made a move toward us and I thought it was round one. Instead he just spit on the ground and headed for the Ranger Shack.

Digger said, "Sonofabitch left before I could use 'em all."

Just about that time, one of the Tobanites we called "The Sidewinder" came toward us. The Sidewinder was a short guy who looked even shorter because he was slightly stooped over. He had a thin face and an oversized nose, which was so thin he coulda used it to pick locks. His hair was all gray and looked like a toilet brush that got caught in a garbage disposal. He got his sidewinder designation by the way he walked. He would bear left until he ran out of real estate and then stop and re-orient himself. When he walked down the dock we always waited for him to go off the side. Like Ellen's ash, it never happened.

The Sidewinder was Dr. Parker, a research chemist and one of those people who looked with their teeth. When he read anything, he would squint his eyes and bare his front teeth. He had glasses that looked like a storm window turned sideways. A head wind would have him marching in place. Whenever he came around, we would give him something to look at. He never caught on.

He had to be smart, why else would he be sporting an Einstein hairdo?

One time, The Sidewinder was in a hurry to catch up to Sam and he actually broke into what was a run for The Sidewinder. He looked like Walter Brennan out for a jog.

The Sidewinder decided that he would invite Libby, the sweet Hostess, over for a romantic meal at his cabin. Libby was the quintessential southern belle. She looked totally out of place on the Island. She must have needed a job and knew someone at the NPC headquarters in Kentucky. She had perfectly coiffed hair, wore a different dress every night, and spoke with a thick, sexy southern accent. Libby was no spring chicken but she looked good and was very guarded about her age.

It was all set. The Sidewinder picked Libby up on her day off and whisked her off to his cabin in Tobin Harbor. It was a pretty crummy day, with wind and rain pelting down. No matter, Libby stepped on the boat decked to the nines and they disappeared around the point.

The weather report was for rain and high winds, but The Sidewinder said he just had to go around Scoville Point. Most of the two miles to Scoville was protected by outer islands. Besides, The Sidewinder assured us, this wasn't his first boat ride.

Later that night, we were sitting in the employee dining room when the door flew open and there was Libby, soaking wet, shivering, bleeding from a head wound, and crying hysterically. She was trying to tell us that they had been blown on the rocks near Scoville Point. Between sobs, she said The Sidewinder was clinging to the rocks, holding on for dear life.

It was obvious Libby was really hurting and we helped her to the nearest bed and wrapped her in blankets. Lurch went to get Sam and find out if there were any doctors in the house.

Four of us took off toward Scoville Point. The trail didn't

always stay next to the shore and we had to take a lot of side trips to make sure we didn't go past The Sidewinder. The first thing we saw was his boat broken in two with the back half bobbing around with the motor still attached.

I got to The Sidewinder first. He was lying on the rocks, crying for help. I wanted to kick him in the ass for what he did to Libby, but he looked pathetic lying in the fetal position, crying and whining.

After some examination, we determined that he hadn't broken anything. We helped him up, wrapped him in a blanket we brought, and led him back to the Lodge.

Sam was in the Emp dining room and said the doctor was with Libby. Sam said the doc thought Libby may have broken her back. Now I really wanted to kick The Sidewinder in the ass. Libby ran about a mile and a half with a broken back! She proved to be one tough Southern Belle.

Once again, Sam called Ned to be there at first light to get Libby. Because of Libby's broken back, Sam got the Park Service to okay a one time Rock Harbor landing for the *Goose*. It would be too tough to carry Libby over the ridge and down the hill to Tobin Harbor.

The plan was to run the *Goose* up on a small beach in front of the dining room and carry Libby on a stretcher to the passenger door. The stretcher bearers would have to wade some as the passenger door would still be in the water.

We would have to push the *Goose* off the beach, and I was going to tow the *Goos*e out to the middle of Snug Harbor where Ned was going to fire her up and take off.

Libby was hurting like hell and if it wasn't for the shot of morphine, I am not sure she could have made it. Everything went as planned and I still wanted to kick that kot-damn Sidewinder in the ass.

Libby spent the rest of the summer in traction at the hospital on the mainland.

Whenever the *Ranger III* was due, a crowd gathered on the big dock, and Oarlocks was always talking to a tourist while they both waited. His current victim was wondering about the formation of the numerous outer islands and how they made a protective barrier for all of Rock Harbor.

Oarlocks explained that this was no accident. In fact, Oarlocks said that as proof, one can see how perfectly straight they were arranged. During the thirties, one of the WPA projects under the Roosevelt administration was to shield Rock Harbor from the ravages of the Big Lake. The outer islands were created by workers blasting and piling the rocks on underwater cribs. They secured the underwater cribs to the main island with huge underwater cables.

Oarlocks was quick to add, "Don't expect the Park Service to admit to this, because they are afraid of sabotage and even the ones that know about it, won't say a word."

I learned early in life that if you say something with authority, no matter how ridiculous, someone will believe you.

Haapala wasn't the only one that had no mercy for seasick Toads. If Oarlocks was around when a boat load of Greenies landed, he would pick one out and ask, "Can you imagine the crossing Chris Columbus had?"

Most Toads could barely stand up, much less answer questions. About all they could muster was to give Oarlocks a quizzical look. Oarlocks went on, "Do you know the first thing Columbus asked his First Mate after they landed?"

Oarlocks didn't wait for an answer. "Columbus turned to his First Mate and asked, 'Is it me, or does it feel like we are still on the boat?'"

While we were waiting for a boat, there was usually a break

in the action for Lurch and me. During one of those lulls, it struck me that Donnie had a fifteen horse Evinrude just like my second motor. I wondered how fast my boat could go if I used both motors.

I had to take a couple of transom bolts off so that both motors would fit, and I could still turn them. The combined weight of the motors and me made the bow point up at a 45° angle and the top of the transom was about an inch above the water.

When I twisted both throttles wide open, the *Sisu* almost went airborne. When the bow flattened out, Digger swore the motors were the only thing in the water. Dudley was standing outside the Smokey station as I went by the *Ranger III* dock at a high rate of speed. The *Sisu* was hell to steer holding both tillers and trying to look forward. Compounding the steering problem was the fact that both props turned in the same direction. Normally, on a boat with twin outboards, the props turn in opposite directions to neutralize the torque forcing the boat to go hard left.

Digger couldn't help himself, as he turned to ask Dudley, "Want to go for a ski?"

Dudley went back into the Smokey shack presumably to check whether there was any violation he could find to charge us with.

It was actually better if there was someone else in the boat to hold the bow down. It was tough to steer empty as most of the boat was out of the water. We spent a few hours taking some of the off duty Emps for a ride bee-lasting all around Snug Harbor.

Two days later, the Park Service installed a buoy in the middle of Snug Harbor proclaiming 10 MPH/NO WAKE.

There was no resident clergy on Isle Royale, so the Catholic Church arranged to have the Michigan Tech priest, Father McGuire, conduct services on the Island. I developed a casual friendship with the Father and always enjoyed talking to him.

I was struck by how young and good looking he was. Strange,

that a guy like him would swear off women for life. Father McGuire was usually accompanied by one or more Nuns. Seemed like a nice gesture - a kind of road trip for the Nuns.

One Saturday night, I was returning from a moonlight ride with Kathy and I saw Father McGuire leaving the Nuns' room. Since it was past 2am, I asked him if he was ok.

In fact, Father said, "I locked my key in my room, and wondered if you could help."

I guess it would be less than proper to say the Father was shit-faced, but he was. I didn't want to wake up a housekeeper and I always left my pass key in the office, so I walked the Father to his room and tested the windows. The bathroom window wasn't locked (why anyone would lock anything on the Island is a puzzlement). I crawled in and opened the door. I got a "Bless you son" as Father McGuire stumbled toward the closet.

The next afternoon as we were loading the passenger's luggage for the trip to the mainland, I saw the Father and the Nun walking toward the dock. I hadn't seen them when they arrived on Saturday, but even through her swaddling clothes, one could see she was nothing short of beautiful. I will leave this subject here and you may draw your own conclusions. As Roy (that would be Roy Rogers) would possibly counsel the priest, "Let your conscience be your guide and may the good Lord take a likin' to ya."

Chapter 5

FIRE IN THE HOLE (ACTUALLY THE GUEST HOUSE)

During one of the *Ranger III* days, after Lurch and I had everyone in their rooms, we were unloading the luggage. A thin, unassuming, older man approached me and asked if I could give him a hand when I was through with the luggage. I assured him I would be back in about twenty minutes to help him.

When I returned, he was standing on the dock with a rather large propane powered refrigerator next to him. "Unusual luggage container," I remarked.

He said, "I'm Wes and I need to get this refrigerator up the harbor about a mile to my cottage."

The fact that he had a cottage on the Island meant he was an original Islander. I asked him if he had given any thought to how we would accomplish this, considering we were both pretty thin and the trail was pretty rugged. He said he thought we could lash a couple of the Concession scows together, put some boards across both boats and run it up the harbor via water. He said he was an engineer by trade.

I got the two widest wooden scows and tied them together

with rope. I put a motor on one of them and laid some boards across and lashed them to each boat. The refrigerator was a lot heavier than an electric model due to the propane motor that drove the compressor. Next, we dragged the boat without the motor onto the shore and created a ramp from the shore to the gunnel. We lashed the refrigerator to a two wheeled cart and rolled it up the ramp onto the boat.

We got the boats floating with the reefer aboard. It was some sight to see us going down the harbor with two boats and a reefer lashed between them.

I gently beached both boats in the small rocky cove he called "Coffee Pot Landing" where his cottage was built. We built a ramp from the rocks to the boat and wrestled the ice box onto land. We then used our hand cart to move the refrigerator along the boards until we got it to the cottage steps. In no time, the refrigerator was in the cottage, hooked up to the propane tanks, and starting to cool a six pack of beer he had stored in his cottage. He said I deserved the first cool one from the fridge, and I wasn't going to argue.

We had a great conversation of what life was like on the Island when he spent the summers there. When he spoke about the Park Service takeover, he got quite serious and didn't say much, except for that he and his family resented the way they took over.

He and I drank a beer and I went back to the Lodge with the two scows. I ran into him from time to time and when his vacation was finally over, he went back on the *Ranger III* for the return trip home.

Some time later, I found out that Wes was actually Wes Farmer, whose family built and ran the Rock Harbor Lodge. Wes and his father Weston built the original Guest House which comprised the original Lodge. The Guest House had indoor plumbing, which was a first on the Island.

The Guest House is the most historic buildings left on the Island, and was built in 1928, and was operated by the Farmer family until the Park Service took over in 1946. It was two stories tall and had about sixteen guest rooms. As I mentioned before, on the first floor there was a lounge with a fireplace large enough to house a Buick Roadmaster. There were double doors on both sides of the lounge. One set of doors served as the main entrance to the Guest House and the other set led out to a large deck that extended over the Lake.

Occasionally, someone would request to stay in one of the Guest House rooms. These people were always old timers that wanted to relive a magical visit from their younger days.

Kathy and I spent many hours on the deck and in the lounge. Once or twice, when desire short circuited the logic portion of our brains, we snuck into one of the rooms. They were still furnished like they were in the '30's and '40's. The only downside was the night watchman. He roamed the Lodge area like a zombie. He even kinda looked like one. It didn't happen often, but now and again he would check all of the rooms in the Guest House. It never happened when Kathy and I were in one, thanks to the Island Gods.

Later that summer, Weston, Sr.'s wife Bea and son Jerry came out to the Island for a vacation. Bea was much more communicative than her son Wes, and she was chuck-full of Island stories of what life was like, pre Park Service.

Bea ran both the Rock Harbor Lodge and the resort on Belle Isle. Belle Isle was on the north side of the Island and sported a nine-hole, par three, golf course. All of the dirt on the course was imported and several greens are still visible.

In order to provide the best meals possible, Weston bought the land seven miles southwest of Rock Harbor known as Daisy Farm. Daisy Farm was a sizeable settlement for early miners and loggers. It is one of the larger flat areas on the Island and is capable of docking deep draft vessels.

Weston intended to grow fresh vegetables on the only land with (barely) enough top soil. The experiment was a bust, especially the root vegetables. The carrots were about two inches long and fat. Potatoes looked more like large shooter marbles and would have taken quite a few to adorn even one plate.

Bea was not as silent about her criticism of the National Park Service as both Weses were. Listening to some of her stories removed any remorse we may have had for causing havoc among the National Park Bureaucrats. The Park Service established a price for the privately owned property and buildings and there was no negotiating. The price they established was dimes on the dollar for what they were actually worth.

Bea also confirmed the stories of burning fishermen's homes, sometimes with the entire family watching. She said her father became so enraged with the Park Service, that he set out for Houghton, Michigan in a small boat and arrived semi-conscious, near death.

I learned from Bea that Wes was a naval architect and founded a well-known mechanics magazine. One of his credits was working on the design of the PT Boat used in World War II. I was always amazed to meet some of the most unassuming, accomplished people in the United States on Isle Royale.

There are days on the Island that are as perfect as a summer day can get. The converse is also true. It was a particularly dreary stretch of several days and I ended up covering for two other Concession workers. One was sick, and the other had a day off to return to the mainland.

Two old ladies were staying for a week and their daytime hobby was to drive me crazy. They couldn't do much other than hang around the Lodge. They did manage to find the Guest

House lounge with its enormous fireplace, which was an ideal place to spend a cold and rainy afternoon.

The ladies went to my boss and asked if there wasn't someone who could start a fire in the guest house fireplace. Sam turned the assignment over to me. I never turned Sam down for anything as he was one of the only people keeping me from a one way trip home.

Once the ladies knew the identity of the fire builder, it became an every day chore. "Sonny, say Sonny, can you please light a fire in the Guest House?" This required making kindling, hauling wood and tearing up the entire Sunday "Detroit Free Press", not to mention the periodic feeding of the behemoth that, even dampered down, could go through a half a cord an hour.

After the third fire, the entire fire thing was getting old. It didn't matter that I introduced myself. They still insisted on calling me "Sonny." This time I told them I was busy, but if they would show up at precisely ten this morning, I would have a fire going.

First, I chopped enough kindling to cross pile the rows two feet high with space between each piece to allow maximum circulation, across the entire fireplace. The kindling was stacked on enough paper to cause a pulp factory to add a second shift. Next, I stacked another two feet of dried, split hardwood. Finally, the coup de grace: one gallon of kerosene poured on the paper and kindling.

The ladies were right on time and I threw a match on the kerosene, and left via the back door, and snuck around the side to watch the action. As the blue-haired pair entered the lounge, the kerosene was just getting started.

The two old pyro fans were nodding their approval at the perfect-looking fire. It didn't take too long for the kerosene, fed with oxygen and kindling, to begin to burn with vigor. In short order, the fire began to omit a low roar. The blue-hairs were glancing at each other at bit nervously. Soon, the low roar was replaced by a loud roar.

The blue-hairs were struggling to get off the Guest House couch as their hair was within the "singe zone." They were beginning to panic and I was beginning to worry as well.

The fireplace was transformed into a Bessemer converter and the built up creosote in the chimney added to the flames and roar. All I needed was a cauldron and some pig iron, and I could have made a batch of steel. In all of the pictures of steel mills, the guys near the fire have shields and asbestos suits. The ladies' attire contained no asbestos.

The ladies ran and one of their heels got caught in the steps causing her to fall into the mud puddle at the bottom of the stairs. I wasn't laughing. Neither lady was hurt or suffered any burns. Thanks for that, but there was still the issue of the Guest House going up in flames. If that happened, they would want names.

I backed off to see the flames coming out of the top of the chimney which was three stories high. Luckily, it had rained for three days or the north end of the island would have been on fire. As it was, I was seeing the original Rock Harbor Lodge building, which had been put on the National Historic Register, going up in flames.

One huge piece of luck came into play. The Park Service had just installed a pipe line all around Rock Harbor, complete with fire hydrants. This would be the first test of the system.

I ran to the Smokey house and rang the fire bell. They came-a-running, hooked up the brand new fire hose, and turned the system on. It worked! They hosed down the outside of the chimney which was shooting flames fifteen feet above the three story chimney!

By now, the fireplace was dialed to "max" and I estimate it was running at two to three cords per hour. This was also fortunate, as most of the wood I had piled into the maw, was burned up. The consensus from the Smokeys was that the creosote was built up inside the chimney and caught fire. I agreed.

Thankfully, the ladies were booked on the *Queen II* leaving later that day. I made sure Lurch took their bags to the boat. They did ask for the boy that started the fires for them. Lurch gave them some excuse for my absence, but I did wave good bye as the *Queen II* pulled away from the dock.

There probably would have been more of an investigation had not Ron Peterson hit a black buoy at dusk with a Smokey's wife on board. No one is saying he was fooling around with her, but he was fooling around with her.

Going from thirty miles per hour to zero in five feet (the amount of feet the bow was compressed) can stop the boat, but anything not bolted down wouldn't fare so well. The Smokey's wife was not bolted down and she French kissed the windshield, which had a detrimental effect on her teeth - almost all of them. Ron told me they looked like a spilled box of chicklets on the floor of the boat.

Ron was just able to run the boat up on the shore by running full throttle and breaking the lower unit in half. Nothing kills an illicit romance faster than hitting a black buoy dead center. The accident took the heat away from us for a while. Both Ron and Smokey Wife had to be flown to the mainland for repairs.

In the meantime, the Park Service inspected the Guest House chimney and said it was good to go. Thanks to the construction employed by the Farmers, the chimney heat didn't get the surrounding wood hot enough to ignite.

I turned over Guest House fire lighting to Lurch. We decided to celebrate the survival of the Guest House with a small fire and party. Everyone was there and Oarlocks was at his best.

Oarlocks was in a philosophical mood and was holding court. He always attracted the young ladies. Oarlocks was expounding on his theories of heaven. He was telling his audience, "I believe heaven is made up of many wonderful things. One of them is a forty acre field covered with tits, and as you run over them barefoot, they squirt scotch and soda."

Anyone else telling the story would have been promptly reported to the management. Oarlocks was regaled with laughter and you could tell everyone wanted more.

I regarded Oarlocks as a good friend and he told me on more than one occasion he felt the same about me.

I made a few bets with a couple employees and Smokeys that Oarlocks was a college graduate. It wasn't hard to reel them in for a quick five bucks. As soon as the bet was made, I ran up to the room and returned with his framed diploma - a masters degree at that.

The moose population on the Island fluctuates from six hundred to a thousand, depending on the severity of the winter and the number of wolves. Usually, there are from thirty to forty wolves that really get hungry in the winter.

If it wasn't for the wolves, there would probably be ten thousand moose all about three feet tall - Shetland moose.

Besides asking for booze or beer, the second most asked question by tourists was: "Sonny, where can I go to see some moose?"

Once again, the Lord delivered the enemy into my hands. My standard answer was, "You can try hiking the trails for a hit or miss encounter, but…. for a small fee, you can get a boat ride and a guaranteed moose sighting."

I seldom got turned down and I would take them up Tobin Harbor through Merritt's lane before sunset to a small lake just inland from the Merritt Lane campsite. There was always at least one big Bull Moose wading in the lake, eating lily pads and whatever other vegetation grew in the lake.

One day, Digger and I were cruising along Merritt Lane on the way to one of our favorite fishing spots and that damn Bull Moose was swimming across the lane to a small outer island on the other side. I guess he saw some fresh browse he wanted.

Digger said he always wanted to ride a moose and this looked like the perfect opportunity. I pulled along side this wide-eyed humongous bull moose and Digger jumped out of the boat onto his back.

This made the moose very angry. Digger grabbed his horns which made him even madder. I tried to stay next to them, because like the rodeo, once you dismount, there is a good chance the beast will want to make you pay.

Digger said he was satisfied and let go of the horns and grabbed the gunnel of the *Sisu* and swung on board. Bullwinkle was mad as hell and a little scared. We peeled away and headed for home so Digger could get a change of clothes.

Dudley was on the dock when we pulled in. Digger didn't wait for the inquiry. As he passed Dudley, he said "Fell down water skiing," and kept walking.

I was leaving the dock after tying up the *Sisu* when Kurt came running from the dining room. Kurt worked as a waiter in the dining room. He was a good looking guy, but he didn't have a steady girlfriend. He was always on the lookout for tourists and on this day, it seemed like his prayers were answered.

A girl that looked like a movie star came in on the *Ranger III* and Kurt made sure he worked her table in the dining room. Her name was Julie and he invited her to take a moonlit ride with him. Kurt asked if he could borrow the *Sisu*.

Things must have gone well and Kurt was in love. He continued to see Julie for the week she was there. Turns out, Julie came from a famous family in Duluth who were also Isle Royale royalty.

Kurt began sending letters daily, as soon as Julie left for home.

He didn't get a response to the first few letters and figured Julie wasn't interested.

Dennis was the postmaster and in a moment of insanity, he let us open one of Kurt's outgoing letters. We got Kathy to write a steamy response to Kurt. Dennis cancelled the stamp on the "incoming" letter.

Kurt was flying high and wrote an even steamier letter back to Julie. We read that letter and upped the ante one more time. By now, we wondered how Kurt's letters didn't set the paper on fire.

Well, the next letter Kurt received was from Julie's father who threatened to neuter Kurt after he had him fired. We had to keep this stunt among us as we didn't know Kurt's propensity to violence, but we did know messing with the US mail was a federal offense and a big one.

That evening, Kathy and I went to our favorite beach on Scoville Point. We had a cookout, a few beers, some rock wrestling, and finally, a great ride home. We kissed good night and I went up to my room with the anticipation of hearing Oarlocks and his built in chainsaw running full throttle.

As I walked into the room, Oarlocks was sitting up in bed with blood streaming from his nose. Holy Shit! I ran into the bathroom and got a towel. Oarlocks was in trouble and getting weak from the loss of blood. I pressed the towel against his nose and told him to hold it there until I got back with some ice.

I flew to the kitchen where the ice machine was located, grabbed the biggest pot I could find and filled it with ice. I got back to the room and Oarlocks was barely conscious. I wrapped a towel around a handful of ice and pressed it against his nose. I got another towel full and put it behind his neck. This slowed the blood a little and I went to Digger's room.

I told Digger to wake up Sam and ask him if there was a doctor among the guests. Digger and Sam arrived with a first aid kit. There wasn't anything in the kit that was useful in this case. By now, there was blood everywhere. Sam said he checked the guest list and there was a guy in room 232 that was listed as Dr. Perry.

I ran to the room and banged on the door. Dr. Perry answered, and said he was indeed a General Practitioner, and that he would come to see Oarlocks.

I waited for Dr. Perry to get dressed and we went to the room. Dr. Perry got the bleeding stopped and said it looked like Oarlocks ruptured an adenoid. The best he could do was to stabilize the bleeding and get Oarlocks to a hospital ASAP. That wouldn't be until the morning and the best we could do was to radio the mainland and have someone call Ned to bring the *Goose* at first light which, because of our far north latitude, was before five AM.

We all stood by Oarlocks until morning. Digger and I had time to rig a crude stretcher which would take at least four of us to carry Oarlocks to the dock, load him on the boat, and bring him to the *Goose*. This turned out to be a feat tougher than bringing the refrigerator to the Farmer's cottage.

Oarlocks was able to move a bit by the time we got him to the *Goose* and we laid him in the aisle between the seats. Dr. Perry and I went with Oarlocks, and Sam arranged to have an ambulance waiting at the airport when we landed.

We got Oarlocks into the ambulance, and Ned flew the Doc and me back to the Island.

The initial report from the hospital wasn't good. Because of the constant irritation of Oarlocks' adenoids, caused by snoring, they became cancerous. Oarlocks was moved from the local hospital to a larger General Hospital in Marquette for surgery.

The guys on the mainland kept us updated on Oarlock's condition and word was that they got all of the cancer.

One day a very large yacht pulled in from Canada. It was the biggest one for the summer up to this point. The owner was a surprisingly young guy that had a few friends traveling with him. He must have spotted Kathy walking by and invited her to dinner.

She asked me about it and I said, "Hey, it sounds like an adventure you shouldn't pass up." I really didn't think so, but I knew she kinda wanted to go.

It was the longest night I ever had on the Island and I played ping pong and drank beer with one of the Emps that happed to be the Iowa State champion. He kicked my ass every game, but I got better in the process. I finally staggered off to bed and was anxious to see Kathy at breakfast.

I felt very tense when I finally saw her enter the Emps dining room. Keerist that was one good-looking woman. She sat next to me and it wouldn't have taken a PhD in human behavior to see how uptight I was.

I asked, "\How was dinner?'

She said it was nice up to a point. Yacht Boy started getting frisky after dinner and Kathy said she had to go as the hour was getting late. After looking at the clock on the mantel a few times, Yacht Boy finally grabbed it and threw it overboard.

At that point, Kathy said she left and Yacht Boy was not happy. Yacht Boy left that morning and Digger went fishing for a clock. Sonofabitch if he didn't find it! He dried it out and it actually started working. Digger gift wrapped it and put it under my pillow.

I had already planned a cook out on Scoville Point with Kathy and I couldn't wait for the sun to go down. We loaded the *Sisu* with provisions: Vodka, beer, steaks, potatoes, plates, silverware, charcoal, and two pre-made strawberry shortcakes.

I timed our departure close to sundown. As we made our way

to Scoville Point, the sun was setting behind us and the moon was rising in front of us. The moon was full, there was no wind, there wasn't a cloud in the sky, and it was relatively warm. If you can't fall in love under these conditions with the prettiest, smartest woman you ever met, you aren't capable.

The sun extinguished itself in the Big Lake as the moon began rising. The moon was so bright that you could have read a newspaper. We ate steaks, drank beer, fed each other strawberry shortcake, and made out like we met for the first time.

We never noticed that the moon ran its course and the sun made a lap around the planet. As the sun started to rise, we contemplated staying the day, but reality took hold and we packed up and started back.

Thankfully, the sun rises so early that there was no one awake when we got back. We had one last kiss and went off to shower and start our jobs. Not a lot of people had a better night than that one, and I am willing to bet the ranch, Yacht Boy never did and never will.

Chapter 6

SINKING THE BEECH

There wasn't enough business for two regular seaplanes to run daily from the mainland to the Island, so the competition was stiff to say the least. The guy with the twin Beech had an in with the Park Service somewhere and got a license to fly to the Island even though the *Goose* was already established for the second year. Also, courtesy of the Park Service, he got a free float dock next to the *Ranger III* dock in Houghton.

On top of everything, our beer guy on the mainland, Bob Shaw, said the Park Service was acting as an agent for the Beech and never mentioned the *Goose* to anyone interested in a plane ride.

As I mentioned earlier, the Beech pilot was a certified asshole. We called him Beech Boy and he always treated us as his hired slaves to take his passengers to their rooms.

One day, the Beech Boy brought a group of eight people and Lurch had the day off, so I had to meet the Beech and take the people to their rooms. I sold them a couple bottles of booze and got to chatting with one of the leaders of the group.

I mentioned the inherent dangers of retro fitting a plane

designed for wheels with floats versus a plane designed to land and take off on water. The pack leader said they weren't told about the *Goose* when they were looking to fly to the Island. I told him I could work a package deal for them to fly home if they were interested.

The next day, the leader tracked me down and said he was interested in going back on the *Goose.* I had talked to Ned and he gave them a "special" discount if they wanted to go back with him.

The group of eight demanded their money back from Beech Boy for the return trip home. To say Beech Boy was livid still ranks as the understatement of the summer. I could swear liver bile was curling his hair and turning it green.

The next day, Jim Kangas took me aside and said word came down that Beech Boy mentioned that he would personally see that I don't live to see the end of summer. Jim assured me he wasn't just blowing smoke and if he were me, he would exercise extreme caution.

I sat down with Digger to discuss my options and how to counter the threat. I was not taking this lightly as Jim would not have mentioned it if he wasn't genuinely concerned.

The *Goose* anchored to a mooring buoy in Tobin Harbor like a sail boat. The Beech came alongside a small floating dock and tied up like a boat. The people would walk down a ladder onto the dock.

One evening when there was no activity in Tobin Harbor, Digger and I sat on the floating dock and wondered what we could do to thwart the threat. I leaned over the edge of the dock and saw that the facing of the dock was secured to the frame of the dock with huge spikes. The facing went over two feet below the water line to protect the floats on the Beech.

We went to the maintenance shop and grabbed a couple of crow bars and a hammer. We managed to pry a spike out about two inches below the water line. The facing held the spike fast because the wood was swollen as it was under water.

The next day was our day off and we positioned ourselves on the ridge behind the trees so we could watch the floating dock without being seen. Beech Boy always circled once to make sure someone would be on the dock to help tie up and get the passengers and luggage to their rooms.

As Beech Boy nosed the Beech against the dock, there was a loud "pop" as the spike pierced the thin skin of the float. As the momentum of the plane continued forward, the spike was ripping a gash in the float below the water line.

Pandemonium ensued. The passengers were panicking and Beech Boy unleashed a barrage of swear words that would make a Tourett's sufferer sound eloquent. We initially figured the spike would make a small hole in the float and it would allow Ned to pick up a few extra passengers while they fixed the float.

Digger whispered, "I think the kot-damn thing is going to sink." I concurred. Beech Boy lashed the sinking pontoon to the floating dock which tested the strength of his pontoon cleats. They were holding for now.

We were damn glad only the two of us had any knowledge of this one. Digger and I made our way back to the Emp Dining room for a cup of coffee, where there was already a buzz about the Beech sinking.

"No shit," was Digger's astonished reply.

We decided we should go down there and provide our help. It was the least we could do. There were so many people there by now, the floating docks' surface was under water and people were being asked to get off.

Beech Boy, with the help of some Park Service guys, was able to get a temporary patch over the gash and run the plane onto a small beach in Tobin Harbor.

Ironically, Ned had to fly the float repairman and parts out to the Island along with the scheduled Beech passengers for the next couple of days.

The Park Service went over the floating dock with a fine tooth comb and determined that the flexing action of the dock caused the spike to work its way loose.

I mentioned to Jim Kangas that maybe the torn float was an omen and that Beech Boy should give up the idea of killing me. Jim asked, "What are you trying to say?"

I said "Nothing, I'm just saying."

A few days later, Beech Boy told Jim Kangas that he had enough and was leaving after his Saturday run. Jim also said he was still mad enough to kill me.

When Ned heard the news, he brought me a case of Canadian Club "on the house." That particular suit case was pretty heavy.

Ned was busier than ever and he was making two round trips a day more often than not. Digger and I had an open invitation as long as there was an open seat. Most times we went home just for the night.

Digger happened to pick a second flight back that was empty except for him and Ned. I took them both to the *Goose* and waited in the harbor to watch the take off close up. As the *Goose* got up on the step, it seemed Ned was coming right at me. As they went by, I understood why so close: There was Digger's ass hanging out of the co-pilot's window, taking spray at about sixty miles per hour.

Digger definitely retained his "All Pro, Most Valuable Mooner" title. I am pretty sure the FAA and the Smokeys would not have been amused, but I sure was.

Digger returned from the mainland just as a couple of locals came over in their new 28 foot, lap strake, V hulled Cruisers. It was powered by a new 120 horse power Mercury. George Johnson and Stan Mullen came out to the Island to fish and drink for a few days.

They invited Digger and me to have a few beers and swap stories. Well, someone broke out the Canadian Club and it got real drunk out. I stumbled back to the dorm and barely made it to the bathroom where I took the porcelain bus out for a ride. I spent most of the night driving.

Digger stopped by and I told him to tell Sam I was calling in sick. Digger passed the word and the next thing I knew, my nap on the porcelain pillow was interrupted by a knock on the door. Thinking it was Digger, I opened the door and there was Sam with some Alka Seltzer. To my surprise, he was chuckling as he mixed the antidote.

Then Sam said, "Don't wallow with the pigs at night if you can't soar with the eagles the next day."

I told Sam it was advice well-taken and further, "I felt like I was shot at and missed, then shit at and hit."

I couldn't move from the room for the entire day and didn't feel all that good the next day. I ventured back to see if George was still on the Island and the boys had a good laugh at my expense.

George and Stan had to get back to the mainland and the weather was not conducive to crossing with their boat. They opted to go back on the *Goose* and asked if I would take care of the boat! Would I? Christmas came twice this year. George cautioned me not to let anyone else near the boat unless I was there as he tossed me the keys.

George knew me and my family forever and I knew his. One other important part of the equation, I'm sure, was that we were both Yoopers.

After the *Sisu*, George's boat seemed like a yacht. Kathy and I spent all of our off hours touring, fishing and sight-seeing places we would have had a hard time getting to with the *Sisu.* One of the best features was the absence of oarlocks.

George was also considerate enough to leave four cases of beer under the floor boards. I figured it was fair payment for a storage fee.

One of the first places I took Kathy was to visit Pete Edisen. He was a commercial fisherman who still had a license to net fish. I think there was only one other netting license. Pete would supply the Lodge with the best whitefish I have ever tasted.

Pete was Isle Royale. Pete, like many characters I met, could easily command their own book. Pete was such a kind, gentle, loving man, even the critters knew. As we approached Pete's dock, he was standing in his yard with a seagull perched on his head.

He spent most of his life on the Island and was one of the few that had stayed on the Island during the winter. Once you made that commitment, you were on your own from November until April. Peter Oikarinen captured Pete's quote in his book, "Island Folk," regarding winter on the Island. "It's beautiful. Finest thing a man can do is stay a winter on this Island." Spending a winter on the Island is not for the faint of heart. NPS headquarters is located on Mott Island, which was named for Charles Mott who succumbed to an Isle Royale winter. The supply ship never made it due to the November gales, and Charles and his wife were left on their own. Only his wife managed to barely survive.

We arrived at Pete's dock and as he approached, the seagull hopped off his hat. One thing you could always count on was nonstop story telling by one of the greatest story tellers I have ever heard.

The seagull stayed as close to Pete as he could and still stay away from us. Pete told us the story of when he was asked by the

Park Service to "acclimate" four wolves they brought to the Island to help control the moose population.

Pete went on, "It was a hot day in July, around seventy degrees, and the alpha wolf I named Jimmy looked awful thirsty. His tongue was hanging out and he was panting. I filled an aluminum pot with water and stuck it through the fence. Jimmy walked over to the pot and proceeded to chew it up like a soda cracker." Pete was laughing at the memory.

I asked Pete how he fed the wolves. He showed me a stick about two and a half feet long that was hanging on the porch above his head. He said he brought the food into the pen in one hand and the stick in the other. A couple of times Jimmy bared his teeth and came at Pete with bad intentions.

Pete said that is where the stick came in. He said when Jimmy got close, he would stick the stick down his throat. Pete chuckled as he said, "It's hard to bite me when you have a stick down your throat."

Pete got serious when he recalled the day the Park Service decided to release them into the wild. The Park Service had no way to transport them to a remote part of the Island and just opened the pen and shooed them away. Instead of running off into a remote area of the Island, the wolves hung around the Rock Harbor area and began terrorizing the tourists.

The Park Service made the decision to shoot the wolves and succeeded in killing three of them. Jimmy eluded the shooters and Pete swore he lived to a ripe old age in a secluded area of the Island.

About that time, Pete's wife was calling him. He apologized and said his wife was awful sick. I was glad Kathy got to meet a true legend.

The 120 horse Mercury was one thirsty sonofabitch. George had a forty gallon auxiliary tank in the form of a barrel secured in the middle of the transom. Every time I filled it up, which was fairly often, Digger would stumble on his way back to the gas pump and hit the handle that caused the pump to reset and show all zeros on the display. Digger apologized for not being able to charge me as the damn pump spun back before he was able to get a number.

It was lucky Beech Boy left. A few days after he took his ball and bat and went home, Ned was firing up the *Goose's* twin 450 horsepower Pratt and Whitney engines and the port engine caught fire. Ned opened the pilot side window and leaned out with his fire extinguisher and put the fire out. He turned back to the plane full of people, and said, "No need to be alarmed; it happens a lot."

Before starting the engines, Ned primed them until gas poured out of a small vent at the bottom of each engine. I often wondered why they didn't catch fire more often. I told Ned I would sit in the harbor to take pictures of the *Goose* as it took off. As I looked through the view finder, the *Goose* got bigger and bigger, and I think I missed the last few shots I had planned as I was laying in the bottom of the boat.

On several occasions, when the *Goose* wasn't full, I went home to see the folks and replenish the booze supply. Beer was no problem, but booze was always tougher to get and I was mostly on my own.

I was walking near the Smokey Station one day when Dudley rushed out of the door and headed straight toward me. Naturally, my first thought was, "What is Dudley going to hammer me about now?"

"Good morning, Dudley," I said in my cheeriest voice. "What's on your mind?" I bit my tongue before adding, "besides dust."

"Well, I wonder if you could ask Ned if I could hitch a ride back to the mainland with him? My folks are coming to town and I wanted to spend a few days with them on the mainland."

I told Dudley I was sure Ned would be happy to take him if there was room, but I would ask anyway.

Ned said there would be no problem if there was room and as luck would have it, I was going to the mainland to shop for clothes. Kathy was kidding me about my wardrobe. I didn't say anything to her, but I was about to go styling.

Ned had to make two trips that day and on the second trip back, there was only me and Dudley on board. It was a gorgeous evening when we took off and the sight of the Island disappearing in the low sun was spectacular. Ned seemed to be flying at a higher altitude than usual, but I figured he wanted to give us a great view.

Ned said he wanted to show us what a *Goose* could do and he put it into a straight down dive! Holy crap! I was scared shitless, but didn't show it. I looked back at Dudley and he was looking out the window and screaming. We dove for what seemed like forever before Ned started pulling it out of the dive. I couldn't see how fast we were going, but I am sure it bordered on the outer limits of what the *Goose* could stand.

Dudley could barely walk when we landed and I gotta admit I was a little shook myself. Ned had a wry smile and I could read his mind. Dudley did say he was taking the boat back to the Island with his folks.

Whenever I got a chance to go back to the mainland, I gave my Mom cash and she would send Piggy a check with a balance sheet that showed how much I still owed. If I couldn't get home, I would send Piggy a money order from the Post Office with updated accounting. Correspondence was only one way. At least Piggy knew my name as I signed each payment sheet.

I had a suitcase full of booze on this trip back. When we

landed in Tobin Harbor, and as Ned was tying the *Goose* to the buoy, he noticed a rather large welcoming party. It included the Park Superintendant, Jim Kangas and Sam, waiting on shore under and behind trees just off the dock. Since there were only two of us on the plane, it was pretty evident the boys figured they were going to catch me red-handed with the booze.

They would have scored a two pointer as they would have finally been able to get me off the Island and they would have been able to revoke Ned's permit, which would have cleared the way for the Beech Boy.

Ned stayed on board with the booze, and when I got on the dock, I unzipped my overnight bag and opened it up as I walked past the welcoming committee without saying a word. Later, Sam told me that my theatrics only served to piss off the Superintendant and deepen his resolve to get me off the Island.

Ned, bless his heart, said he had to run down to Vindigo-kot-damn (he really didn't have to), so he was firing up the *Goose* before I hit the dock. Since the *Goose* loved gas like the Devil loves sin, that trip cost him more than a few cases of booze.

We both agreed it wasn't worth the gamble to bring any more booze on the *Goose*. Ned said he would have a hard time explaining to his partners that he was thrown off the Island because of a rum running operation.

Jim took me aside and said that he had no chance to warn me about the welcoming party since it was sprung on him that morning. He also confirmed that I was way too cocky and that I still had a bulls-eye on my back as far as the Park Service was concerned.

I was more convinced than ever that the group overseeing our time on earth was still keeping me from harm. I just didn't know why.

The first thing I did was look up Kathy to model my splendid sartorial ensemble. I had a checkered Hathaway shirt, the latest cuff-less slacks, wax hide loafers, and an eye patch. The eye patch was always worn by the guy on any Hathaway advertising.

Kathy was blown away. I told her it was easy to be at the top of the fashion fad, it just took money. She wasn't all that materialistic, but was still impressed. We made plans for a Scoville Point cookout and I said I would wear my new outfit, sans the eye patch.

I was still supplementing my income by betting on various stunts. One of these involved a skill I became very good at executing. When we met the Voyaguer, we had to back the tractor with the luggage trailer down a very long, narrow wooden dock. Backing the trailer took a touch that Lurch hadn't mastered and when I wasn't available to meet the boat, Lurch would unhook the trailer and walk it to the end of the dock and then back the tractor down the dock.

I made a bet one night that I would lock the tractor throttle in the wide open position and back the trailer down the dock full blast. Everyone wanted a part of that bet as they really wanted to see me and the tractor go into Snug Harbor.

Digger collected about a hundred dollars in bets and side bets to see this one. If I cut the throttle before I got to a line near the end of the dock, I lost. If I went into the drink before I got to the line, I lost.

The moment of truth: Holy Shit! It felt like I was going a hundred miles an hour. I made it! I told Digger to mark that one down as a "one time only." The "one time only" list was growing.

One night we were sitting in the Emp dining room and fell prey to the "mouth overloading one's ass" syndrome once again. I declared that for a small wager, I would eat a number ten can of pineapple in thirty minutes. A number ten can is an institutional size that can feed a decent size village in China with leftovers.

Thankfully, Digger only collected about thirty bucks for this one. You cannot imagine how many f****ing pineapple rings there are in a number ten can. I know now. I got carried out on my shield on this one. Digger also lost money on this one as he believed if I made the bet, I would win.

Chapter 7

KILLING DENNIS
and
ANGEL UNAWARE
(With apologies to Roy Rogers and Dale Evans)

Lake Superior has a very small tide of about an inch, but I did notice that periodically, the water in the harbor would fluctuate almost a foot. None of the Smokeys could explain this and some were even skeptical that it occurred.

The University of Rhode Island had a research boat with marine science students studying Lake Superior for the summer. I told the Captain about my observation and he said that the lake level does indeed fluctuate, but it wasn't the tide. It was due to something called a seiche (pronounced saysh), derived from the French word that means "to sway back and forth." He went on to say that lake level changes occur when there was a significant difference in barometric pressure from one end of the lake to the other. Another possible cause could be high winds that push water higher on one end, lowering the level on the other. I also noted that a seiche would last at least half an hour most times.

By monitoring NOAA forecasts that the Smokeys put on the

bulletin board every day, you could almost forecast a seiche. The reports had very specific data regarding barometric pressure and wind velocities across Lake Superior. This gave me an idea for making a few bucks.

Across from the *Ranger III* dock sat the old *Ranger II* dock which was made of wood and was used by private boats when there was no room at any of the finger docks. A part of the dock jutted out into Snug Harbor and there was a small opening underneath.

Under normal conditions, the bow of my boat would be about three inches higher that the bottom of the dock. If I ran by wide open, it looked like it was just even with the dock.

I had Digger hype the crowd by saying that for the right price, I would run the *Sisu* wide open underneath the opening. This was no cinch, even with a seiche. Just behind the dock, there was a cluster of enormous boulders and this trick would require making a hard left just after clearing the far side of the dock. All of this would have to be done while lying on my back across the seats and steering the tiller with my hands over my head. No cinch.

Digger managed to raise about eighty dollars in bets, much of it coming from the Smokeys. They wanted to see me hit the dock, rocks, or both. The only condition was that I would pick the time and the day.

I started monitoring the weather reports and got pretty good at predicting seiches. It took several weeks before I felt the moment was right. There was a very large low pressure system at the far eastern end of the Lake, centered on Whitefish Bay. If the theory held, the lake would form a hump under this low and the water in the rest of the lake should be lower.

All the bettors were assembled on the old *Ranger II* dock and I was having second thoughts. The tin *Sisu* could get up to twenty five miles per hour when empty and I would have to execute a turn in less than fifteen feet at precisely the time I cleared the dock.

I never dared a practice attempt, but I did practice steering and making extreme turns while lying down. Digger said he thought this was a hair-brained scheme. I reminded him, "Hell, you gotta take some chances in this life."

For effect, I had Digger positioned, wearing a life jacket in a NPC scow with a life-saving ring and grapple hook.

I made a couple of passes, and then began the live run. I started way out in the harbor and got the *Sisu* aimed straight at the opening. The dock passed over me in the blink of an eye and I threw the tiller to the right as far as it would go. I almost turned her over, and the prop caught one of the rocks. The sheer pin did what it was designed for and sheered in half, and the rock took a bite out of one of the ears on my prop, but I made it. Even the Smokeys applauded, although they weren't as happy when Digger handed me the cash.

We had to make a run to Park Headquarters to retrieve another prop. Jack Jacobs wanted to know how the hell we took a bite out of the prop. Digger gave him a play by play and Jack just shook his head as he gave me a brand new one. He smiled when I gave him a bottle of Canadian Club, his favorite amber liquid.

Dennis was not only the Postmaster, but a damn good photographer. One of the tourists gave me twenty rolls of Kodachrome 35mm color film in lieu of a tip. Since I didn't have a 35mm camera, Dennis agreed to shoot a few rolls for me.

Dennis and I took the *Sisu* through Merritt Lane to get some moose pictures at Hidden Lake. There was a huge bull swimming across the Lane to get to some succulent alder bushes on the other side. Dennis was standing in the front of the boat shooting away and the bull made it to the small island and I was still going full throttle closing fast. I didn't want to cut the throttle suddenly as it would throw Dennis over the bow, and besides, he was getting some great shots.

I guess I stayed on the throttle just a little too long as I ran up on the bank into the alders. Dennis catapulted out of the *Sisu* into the alders which broke his fall and not his camera. Dennis wasn't happy. About all I could muster was "Did you get the shots, Dennis?" I wasn't trying to kill him on purpose, it just seemed like it.

There are days in almost every summer when none of the boats will attempt to cross. Even if they could make it, the adverse publicity generated from the sick passengers would certainly make the crossing a public relations disaster.

This was one of those days. If you looked on the horizon, you could see the mountains. All the old seamen said if you see lumps on the horizon, stay home. The wind had been blowing from the Southeast for two days and the waves crashing on the outer islands sent spray to the tree tops.

Dennis and I had been out in some weather before, but this was the biggest sea we'd seen this summer. The Post Office was closed and Dennis was wandering around on the dock.

"Hey Dennis, wanna go see how big the waves are?"

Dennis replied, "Why not?"

I could think of a few reasons, but this would possibly be a once in a summer event. It would also be a perfect time to challenge the "One-up Prince" from Chicago. His name was Steve Kowolski, and he had been bugging the hell out of me for the past few days. He said he belonged to the Chicago Chapter of the Hell's Angels, and no matter what was discussed, he had done it harder, faster, better, and more often. I asked him if he felt adventurous enough to take a ride on the Big Lake to check out the waves. I made sure there were a few people around so he couldn't back down.

"I'm game for anything," One Upper replied because he had no choice. I was sure he had never been out in any sea even remotely close to the one that was boiling on the Big Lake. It can be terrifying to go down into a wave and see nothing except the wave in front, the wave in back, and the sky. If I figured correctly, this should put an end to the "One-up" stories for the rest of his stay.

Before we got in the boat, I asked him if he had to pass any toughness tests in order to get into the Hells Angels. Naturally, his answer was "Hell yes." I asked him if he was willing to take one more toughness test on the way out to the waves.

"No problem," was his instant answer.

I laid out the challenge: The bet will be a small amount, say ten dollars, which will require him to keep his hand in the water for two minutes.

"Easiest sawbuck I ever made," he replied.

Digger was having a tough time containing himself and had to leave the dock for a few minutes. We made a lot of sawbucks using this bet. No one ever made it even close to one minute, especially with the boat moving. It is the same effect as a wind chill. The water was about forty degrees and when the boat was moving, it felt like forty below. I collected the quick ten dollars and went back to the dock.

We loaded a movie camera and a slide camera in Martin's fourteen foot boat and the Hell's Angel jumped into the *Sisu*. The plan was for me to stand in the boat, holding an oar straight up to see if it would disappear in a trough while Dennis captured the action on the cameras one wave behind.

I could sense Steve's nervousness as we left the dock and Digger was asking if he could have my stuff in the event we didn't return. I told him that he should wait for a respectable time period, like a day before he began pillaging my possessions.

"Have you ever done this before?" Steve asked nervously.

"Not in anything this rough," I chuckled. I knew I had him.

The narrow cut between the reefs was one of the most dangerous aspects of the caper. Because of the shallow reefs between the islands, you had to run a zig-zag course which put you broad-side to the waves.

This was enough for the Hell's Angel, as he was already white-knuckling the gunnels. Even Dennis and I weren't prepared for the size of the waves once we cleared the inner reefs and it was easy to see why the big boats stayed home. The roar from the crashing waves on the outer islands would give anyone pause for thought. One Upper was instantly petrified and began suggesting we go back. I reminded him that he was a Hell's Angel and surely he had faced much more dangerous adventures than this one.

Dennis was signaling for me to hold the oar up, to see if we could measure the waves. I had to wait until we went into the bottom of a trough to get the maximum depth of the waves. I only had a few seconds to let go of the tiller, grab the oar and stand up before the next wave was on us. I did my best balancing act and could see for myself that the waves were above the tip of the oar.

Dennis started shooting from the top of his wave until he got to the bottom and damn near tipped over during the process. I am not sure I could have gotten to him in time.

One Upper was crying by now, and I told him he could lose his Hells Angels'

Membership if the Chapter found out. Besides, I told him turning around was going to be the trickiest maneuver we would face out here. We could ride the waves out indefinitely by heading into them, but if we got broadside at the wrong time, we were going over.

I wanted him to sweat just a little longer, so I kept going away from shore, explaining I was looking for just the right wave. I wasn't feeling too confident in the face of these fifteen-footers that were white-capped at the top. We started taking on water and I suggested to One Upper that he better stop crying and start bailing or the Chicago Chapter would have an opening.

He started bailing, but didn't stop crying. Watching a Hell's Angel putting a death grip on the gunnel, bailing, and bawling made me wish I had the camera. I got to the top of a wave, and signaled to Dennis I was going to turn around. Dennis was running one of the NPC scows and he was having a hell of a time trying to steer and bail.

I got to the bottom of a trough and made a hard left half way up the wave, hoping I could get it turned around before the top of the wave threw us over. I managed to make the turn, but the bow was headed to the bottom of the trough and it isn't where you want to be. The bow digs into the back of the next wave and actually goes under water. When One Upper saw this, I thought he was going to jump out of the boat.

I throttled up, got on the back of the wave and rode it all the way into the cut. Dennis managed to get around and was headed for home a couple of waves behind us. As we headed back to the dock, I noticed One Upper's pants were wettest in the crotch area. He noticed my glance and immediately passed it off to one of those big waves that crashed into the boat. I figured he was sufficiently humiliated and let him have this one. I suggested that he use some of the water he was bailing and accidently spill it on himself.

There was quite an audience assembled when we got back. Everyone wanted to know what it was like. One Upper remained mute. One of the girls noticed his red eyes and wet pants and asked One Upper if he was scared. One Upper just shook his head and headed for his room.

Dennis and I planned to make the Tuesday beer run to Mott Island. The night was clear and the moon was full. It was one of those nights where they take the moon shots over water and use it in a calendar.

Befriending some of the Park Service Personnel that had access to the beer boat was our top priority. It didn't hurt that some of our friends from a prior life worked at Mott Island and were willing accomplices in our quest for the nectar of the vats.

I had lent the *Sisu* to Digger for a long-planned date and had to borrow Donny's twelve foot cedar boat. The plan was simple, take Donny's boat to Mott Island, pay a small premium for Milwaukee's finest, return to home base to consume some, and sell some to pay for the next shipment. There was one complication for this run, however. The Park Service had just passed an edict (aimed directly at us) that anyone caught at night without running lights would be prosecuted to the full extent of the law. That posed a problem, as we couldn't pull up to the Lodge with ten cases of beer in broad daylight and Donny's boat didn't have any running lights.

We decided that we would be violating fewer and less important laws by running at night, than parading around with contraband during the day. In preparation to skirt the running light rule, we took Donny's boat about a quarter-mile down the harbor to the Farmer's beach - "Coffee Pot Landing." It isn't on any map, but if the Farmer's named it, it was good enough for the rest of us. Coffee Pot Landing was a fifteen-foot wide collection of mostly smaller rocks. After dark, the plan was to walk to Coffee Pot Landing and launch from there.

We pushed off at about ten that night, when it finally got dark enough for smuggling. Donny's boat had a small deck across the bow. Dennis decided to sit on the bow facing backward to protect himself from the wind. This would prove to be a fateful decision.

I couldn't see directly in front of us because of Dennis, but the moon was so bright, I could see that I was traveling straight as a die and a safe distant from both shores. We were about halfway to

Mott when it seemed like we took a direct hit from some off-shore shelling exercise. I actually thought that we may have been hit by a meteor. The impact drove my ass through a one-inch thick oak seat. I was sitting on the bottom of the boat, trying to steer with the tiller directly above my head.

I was looking around for Dennis, and suddenly I heard an inhuman cry screaming, "STOP THE BOAT, STOP THE BOAT". I twisted the throttle to stop. Dennis was on the outside of the boat with a death grip on the gunnel.

I grabbed Dennis and he started screaming louder. I picked him up under the arms and sat him in the boat. It was another one of those times you don't think about anything and adrenalin takes over and gives you inhuman strength.

Dennis was in shock and bleeding from the back of his head. The blood was streaming down his neck and he was babbling. I splashed some water on his face and slapped him a couple of times like I saw Jimmy Cagney do in a movie. He finally regained his composure and asked what the hell happened. What happened was we hit a boat head on!

I found an old towel in the boat; dipped it in the lake, wrung it out and pressed it on Dennis's wound. I told Dennis to hold it on the wound and he said he couldn't raise his right arm. I guess that is one of the reasons God gave us two.

Dennis said his shoulder hurt like hell. That wasn't too surprising since our combined speed was about 50 miles per hour.

It was amazing Dennis held on. Dennis said he had to hold on since he didn't know how to swim! Given that he had a heavy Coast Guard issued jacket that weighed about a hundred pounds when wet, it was amazing he survived. Once again the Park Superintendant in the Sky intervened, or so it seemed.

I turned around and started looking for the other boat and/

or survivors in the water. It was a Park Service boat and Don Peterson was piloting. There were four other people on the boat and miraculously, no one was injured. After we assured each other that everyone was okay, we checked the damages. Our little cedar boat had a small chunk out of the bow and the Park Service boat, the *Tobin*, a twenty-two foot aluminum boat with twin outboards, sustained a hellacious dent in the hull. The *Tobin* was Dudley's boat for the summer and Don borrowed it to go to Mott for the same reason we were going there. We hit the *Tobin* two inches left of dead center!

Both boats were going wide open at the time of impact. When we hit, neither bow was in the water, so, we glanced off each other in opposite directions. If either boat was going slower, we probably would have punched a hole in the *Tobin*.

As you recall, Don already had a head-on crash with his boat and a Smokey's wife, so he wasn't eager to have to report another one. Don said he would tell them he hit a dock and that should be the end of the issue. They continued on and so did we. We made it to Mott Island and loaded the beer. Dennis could only watch, as his shoulder hurt so much, he could barely move his arm.

We went back to the Lodge and Dennis realized that his glasses were at the bottom of Rock Harbor. I helped put him to bed and went to the employee dining room for a late night cup of coffee. Don was there and he took me aside and said one of the guys on the boat told Smokey Jim that they hit a boat but didn't see who it was. Don said he blurted it out the minute they hit the dock and there wasn't anything he could do to stop him.

Next morning, I had to help Dennis get dressed and open the post office. I went down to the dock and Jim was at his post at the Smokey Station. He came out to the dock and said one of their boats was hit last night and they had cancelled all days off and put every boat they had in the water to search for the boat that hit theirs. Jim told me there was a little grey paint that rubbed off on the bow of the *Tobin*.

Jim asked if I heard anything that would help him find the culprit(s). I told him that no one said anything to me about hitting a boat. Technically, that was true.

I went to check on Dennis. He was really hurting. I told him I was going to confess to the collision and that he would have to fly back to have his shoulder checked out.

I tracked down Jim and told him to stop looking for the collider. Jim just shook his head and said, "Is there anything that happens on this God Damn Island that you aren't responsible for?"

Then I went to Sam and updated him on the situation. Sam shook his head much like Jim did. I told Sam to radio Ned and see if he could get out here to fly Dennis to the mainland. He did, and Ned said he would leave ASAP.

Dennis swore me in as the temporary Postmaster, which ironically made me the youngest Postmaster in the United States (I was younger than Dennis). There I was: cancelling stamps, answering postal questions, and trying to look official. Meanwhile, the bureaucratic wheels were turning and Jim came to the Post Office to tell me I was in deep shit. The Superintendant intended to prosecute me to the full extent of the law due to the fact that I did some real damage to government property and was operating a boat at night without running lights.

Jim said I was "invited" to the Super's office to fill out the accident report, which would be forwarded to the Keweenaw County Sheriff's office. As soon as I closed the Post Office for the day, Digger and I took the *Sisu* (which had running lights) down to Mott for the meeting with the Super.

We tied up at the front dock at Mott which was unusual since most of the time we were having work done on the boat and had to hide it when Jack worked on it. We were on our way to the

Super's office and I picked up a skip-able rock. I was the champion rock skipper in Rock Harbor and won several contests and money to prove it. I used to tell everyone that we were so poor, I used to get two bags of rocks for Christmas; one with flat ones and one with rounds ones. The flat ones we skipped and the round ones we threw with a sling.

Just then, a seagull flew by and rather than skip the rock I let fly at him. You can never hit a seagull because they have eyes like an eagle and can easily evade a thrown rock. This guy must have been day dreaming 'cause I caught him in the old fish basket and he fell from the sky like a dying duck. I was sure it was his death spiral.

Well, things instantly went from bad to worse. The number two "in charge" Bureaucrat was just coming out of his office when the gull began his downward spiral and splashed in the water about a hundred feet from the dock.

Number Two (our name for him) started hollering, "Did I see you hit that gull with a rock?"

It was then I found out the fine for killing gulls was five hundred dollars, thirty days in the hoosegow, or both. Why they protected these sea going pigeons was beyond everyone except the Bureaucrats. I profusely denied taking the gull out of the air with a rock and told him even a professional pitcher couldn't nail a flying gull with a rock.

Meanwhile the seagull was throwing up and gulping water at the same time.

Number Two would have none of it and said to follow him to the office so he could fill out a violations form. Since I was already there to fill out a violations form, this would make two.

My argument was, "The seagull was going down for a fish and got vertigo or something. I don't think he was hurt so, no harm, no foul."

Number Two said, "Well, let's see how unhurt he is."

We went back to the dock and once again, the Gitche Gumee Gods saw fit to shine down upon me. We looked out over the water and the gull was gone.

One of our Mott pals told us later that the gull took off all right, but made it to the far shore and keeled over between a couple of rocks, toes up.

We went back to the Super's office to fill out the accident report. There was a shit-load of paper work that took about an hour to complete. I signed the report and the Super said I would be hearing from him shortly.

Chapter 8

TWO FISTED JUSTICE

Dennis returned from the mainland with his arm in a sling. His shoulder blade was cracked and he had to immobilize it for a few weeks. The sling was a constant reminder of our ill-fated beer run.

The Super sent the accident report to the Keweenaw County Sheriff, Tom Roberts. He was the only law officer in a county of 541 square miles, and 4 people per square mile. Most of the people were concentrated in a few towns. Everyone knew Tom and vice versa.

When Tom got the accident report, he called my Dad and asked him if he knew Wayne Kallio. My Dad said, "That's my son, What did he do?"

Tom said, "Well, it says here that he hit a Park Service boat head-on at night with no running lights on his boat."

My Dad said, "Is that bad?"

Tom replied, "It's a pretty serious offense, according to the law."

Naturally, my Dad asked, "What happens now, Tom?"

"Well," Tom said, "The bureaucrats all go back to Washington for the winter, which will be in a month or so, and that should end it. In the meantime, I'll file this report in the circular file on the floor here."

My Dad thanked Tom profusely and said he wasn't going to let me know. He said it might act like a behavioral governor.

The head Smokey kept calling Tom to get the status of the case. Tom told him he was still investigating and if he didn't stop hounding him, he would stop investigating. I think the Super knew it was over.

Jack Jacobs had to fix the *Tobin,* which suffered only superficial wounds in the head-on-er. I figured that was worth a bottle of Canadian Club, which I promptly dropped off at Park Headquarters.

Dennis healed quickly and was bragging about not having to grovel at the feet of John Haapala for a hair cut anymore. A couple of Tobin Harborite brothers arrived this week and during a conversation with Dennis, one of them mentioned that he brought his clippers. He would be happy to give Dennis a hair cut if there was a need. Paul and George were from Omaha, Nebraska and Paul's parents had put the Cabin in Paul's name because he was the youngest. Paul and George were both retired and spent their summers in the family cabin in Tobin Harbor.

Dennis accepted Paul's offer and if Dennis hadn't made a big deal about the fact that he was free of John's ritual for good, we may have had some compassion.

Dennis didn't mention the newly acquired hair cut when he first sat down for dinner - he didn't have to. Obviously, there were no mirrors in Paul's place, nor were there any between Paul's place and the employee's dining room. There were clumps of hair missing all over. Some of the missing clumps were shaved clear down to his scalp. It looked like the admissions hair cut for one of the State's Laughing Academies. We didn't crack a smile.

"Dennis," Digger began, "did you get your hair cut?"

"Yea, how is it?" Dennis was oblivious.

"Well," Digger went on, "I am guessing, the clippers didn't work, and since you were there, Paul didn't want to disappoint. So, being from Nebraska, they just happened to have a bull-whip handy. They also had one of those swivel bar stools and while George spun you around, Paul took whacks out of your hair with the bull whip. The other possibility could be that Paul was the head barber in a mental institution."

"You guys just don't know a good hair cut when you see one," Dennis shot back. By now, I went to the kitchen and returned with a mirror, which he held up to Dennis. You never know how sensitive a person is until something like this happens.

Put Dennis down in the sensitive column. He jumped up and ran out the door with the look of a seasick tourist. He wore a cap pulled down tight for the next two weeks.

Oarlocks came back from the hospital and it was obvious he had lost some weight. I went to the room with him to help him unpack and get the full report with no one else around.

Oarlocks had irritated his adenoids so much by the curtain rattling snoring; they became malignant and had to be removed. Since he wanted to get back to the Island before the season ended, he didn't have time to wait for the special plate that would replace his top teeth.

No matter who gets an operation, they can't wait to show you the scar. Oarlocks was no exception. He called me over and opened his mouth wide enough to hold the *Sisu.* He had a hole in the roof of his mouth that was plugged with a chunk of foam that Oarlocks cut from a large piece of foam rubber.

There was a problem. Oarlocks could put the plug in, but he couldn't get it out. That job required stabbing the center of the plug with a slightly open pair of needle nose pliers, gripping the plug, and pulling it out. If you didn't jab the pliers in far enough, you would come away with a piece of foam and a smaller target for the next try. If you jabbed the pliers in too far, you would fork the wound.

Once you got a good grip on the plug, it came out festooned with enough boogers and green matter to gag a maggot on a corpse. That became my job a minimum of once a day. The only positive was that he didn't snore anymore. Once the plug was out, it was almost impossible to understand what Oarlocks was saying. It sounded like he was talking into four echo chambers simultaneously.

No matter what, I had to make sure I was on board before ten every night to get it out. A couple of alternates tried to get it out, but it always ended in disaster. Then I remembered why we called Doc, Doc. Doc was taking pre-med courses on his way to becoming a doctor. He agreed to pull the plug whenever I couldn't. That took a load off my back.

Oarlocks and I would have some philosophical discussions during our nightly plug-pulling sessions. One of his precepts after spending a life time in education was that experience was not transferrable. I am not too sure about that one as he changed the way I felt about several things. He said he came to the conclusion that anger in general was a wasted emotion that took more out of oneself that it did out of the person or thing you were mad at.

Oarlocks had no time for hypocrites. He told me the story about the time he was fishing on a beaver dam from a community raft that someone made and left at the dam. He said he was five-fourths drunk and getting drunker when a member of his former church showed up to do some fishing. This pillar of the church did not know that Oarlocks knew he was a gold plated hypocrite in more than a few ways.

Church Boy started in on Oarlocks by saying how disappointed his parents would be to see him in that condition if they were still alive. Oarlocks responded in true Oarlocks fashion, "I smoke, drink, chew and screw and them's that don't like it don't have to do what I do. Besides, you might want to pick the logs out of your eyes before you start picking the twigs out of mine. For instance, one log might be the time you stepped out with Betty Ann Maher when your wife was out of town at a woman's church convention. That was about the time when Tiny from the party store sold you a bottle of whiskey. I think there are a few more logs on the truck, John."

Church Boy was beating a retreat to his car and Oarlocks was still rattling off his transgressions.

I was in the office talking to the boss when a woman staying in the Lodge came running into the office and was beyond excited. After we got her to calm down a bit she said her husband went for a hike and promised to be back by noon. Here it was five o'clock and he wasn't back yet. Since there are several trails that begin at the Lodge and branch out into many more, we asked her if she had any idea where her husband was headed. She said he mentioned the Greenstone Ridge.

The boss headed straight away to the Smokey Station with the wife and me in tow. Jim said he would dispatch his Smokeys immediately and notify Mott Island for additional help. I volunteered since I was in a lot better shape than Dudley and crew. The Smokeys started out on the trails in Rock Harbor.

I took the *Sisu* to the Three Mile Campground, ah, three miles from the Lodge and started up the trail to the Greenstone Ridge. The trail is a thousand foot rise and about three miles to the Greenstone Ridge. I made pretty good time getting to the Ridge and decided to head toward the far end of the Island. I figured when I got to Mount Ojibway, I could get a pretty good view for miles around and my voice would carry farther from up there.

Just before I got to Mount Ojibway, I saw the guy sitting on the side of the trail looking pretty scared. After our introductions, he told me his foot slipped on a rock and into a crevasse where he twisted his ankle. He had his shoe off and it was swollen, black and blue. We both agreed it was probably broken and moving him was probably more than we could accomplish without more help.

Luckily, there is a trail from Mount Ojibway to Daisy Farm which is across the harbor from the Smokey Headquarters on Mott Island. I took off running, which was a lot easier downhill.

When I got to Daisy Farm, there was a camper there with a boat and he took me to Smokey Headquarters. Luckily, there was a trail crew at Headquarters and they grabbed a stretcher and headed up to Mount Ojibway. They carried the guy like I would carry a case of Kleenix.

They decided to keep the guy at Smokey Headquarters for the night and fly him out the next day. The Smokeys had a small float plane at their disposal, but it was too late to make a round trip.

By the time I got back to the Lodge, it was past ten o'clock and I was beat. The wife and the boss were happy, and so was I.

Chapter 9

GLAZE AT THE MOON, BOYS

A classic management/employee struggle developed about a month into the summer. Management was trying to hold down costs and one of the ways they decided to do it was to feed the employees a prisoners' of war diet.

Were it not for twenty percent unemployment on the mainland, it would be hard to imagine anyone working for the Concession wages on Isle Royale. A non-alcoholic cook that could actually cook was the most valuable employee on the Island.

The cooks were caught in the middle and had to endure the brunt of employee complaints. The management that controlled policy for us may as well have been on the other side of the earth. In effect, they were - the headquarters for the National Park Concessions was in Mammoth Cave, Kentucky. They were righteous enough to ban alcohol, but hypocritical enough to put us on a hostage diet.

Eleana was the head cook and a cross between Mother Theresa and Ghandi. No one didn't like Eleana. Eleana felt terrible about the employee food situation. Her hands were tied and we didn't rag on her.

Only once did we cross the line with Eleana and I regret it to this day. Not only was she the best person anyone ever met, she was also one of the best cooks. Her specialty was apple pie and naturally, the employees were never allowed to do anything but smell it. What a smell that was. If fresh baked apple pie can't start your taste buds bulging, you don't have any. We were allowed leftovers, if the paying guests left any. Fat chance.

Eleana started baking the apple pies at lunch time. We were all drooling while eating our bologna sandwiches on white bread. Bologna sandwiches and watered down tomato soup was the lunch menu five out of seven days. I would like to think this was our main motivation for "appropriating" steaks and other fare from the reefer and dockside store.

The other offering for dinner that night was Isle Royale whitefish. They were caught by Pete Edisen, one of the last two commercial fisherman on the Island allowed to use nets. The Isle Royale variety of whitefish was the most delicious fish I have ever tasted. When you catch a fish with delicate, flaky meat that lives in 38° F water, it is hard to go wrong.

It was a perfect summer day; the big boats were all in port, guests and supplies put away. The evening meal was under control and it was usually a calm time for all employees. We were all standing around the chopping block, with Eleana's fresh apple pies cooling, exchanging the day's trivialities. For some reason, everyone directed their attention to the door and just as they did, I slipped a pie under my bell-hop jacket which was casually thrown over my arm.

While everyone was still watching the door, I saw my chance to make a getaway. "Gotta take a shower," I offered over my shoulder, trying my damnedest not to laugh. In the security of my dorm room, I revealed my treasure to Digger and Donny. We all ate as much as we could and I haven't tasted any pie since then that could even come close. The crust was golden and flaky, and there was a touch of cinnamon and the slightly tart apples battled the sweetness of the sugar. Suffer me.

I would have stored what was left, but Donny saw to it that there was nothing left. In a flash of brilliance, I frisbeed the pie tin into the woods and we went to dinner. There was a furor in the dining room over the missing pie. Sam was about as mad as I have ever seen him. He even took it up a notch when the number of deprived guests came to eight - exactly the number of pieces in a single pie.

The seriousness of the misdeed was illustrated at one AM when The Boss turned on the lights in our dorm rooms for a surprise search and demanded everyone open their lockers. Everyone's room was inspected and the pie tin was redeemable for a one-way boat ride to the mainland. I think The Boss reacted to Eleana's feelings more than the guests' disappointment. Eleana felt personally responsible for the missing pie. Even the rat pack felt remorse for this one; especially me.

The Lodge operated under the American Plan which meant that lodging and meals were bundled under one daily rate. Everyone staying in the Lodge was entitled to three meals a day and non-Lodge guests could purchase any of the three meals a day.

In order to cook this amount of food, there was a head cook, a first, second, and third cook, a baker, and about four or five assistant cooks.

Digger was one of the best at getting under the cooks' skin. One of the ways he would accomplish this was to burst into the kitchen and holler at the top of his voice, "FOOD PLEASE!" This doesn't seem too extreme a measure until you realize he did this at three meals and two coffee breaks - every day. Chinese water torture uses the same principle.

The on-going battle between the Emps and cooks had small skirmishes which became more frequent and raised the tension level all around. Add to that at least five times a day - "**FOOD PLEASE!**" I knew something had to give and this day it finally did.

Digger and I were sitting around in the employee's dining room after dinner having a cup of coffee. On the other end of the room was Ernie, the First Cook, and several of his helpers.

"Digger, you should have been here for supper," I said in a voice extra loud so the entire room could hear. "I couldn't eat the swill we had for supper, so I threw the plateful next to the tree by the back door."

"Coulda gotten charged with trying to kill a tree in a National Park," Digger offered.

"Well, my intention was to feed the gulls, just to solidify our notion that gulls would eat absolutely anything."

"Gull threw up," Digger guessed, keeping his eye on the cooks, who were listening with rapt attention now.

"Nope, gull refused to try it," I replied.

The cooks were starting to squirm in their chairs. I continued, "A squirrel was running up the path and grabbed a mouthful as he ran by."

"Then what?" Digger asked with unmitigated glee knowing this was the set-up question.

Like a finely tuned Vaudeville act, I boomed, "Well, he ran about twenty feet and stopped. He spit out the food, and licked his ass to get the taste out of his mouth!"

Ernie jumped up and hollered, "That does it!" I figured we were in for a couple of rounds, but he ran right by us and out the door.

About five minutes later, The Boss came storming into the dining room and ran right up to Digger and me.

The Boss was six inches from my face, bellowing at the top of his voice, "Ernie just quit and is packing right now for the boat in the morning. I don't know what you said to him to make him quit, but you better hope you can say something to make him stay! If he gets on the boat, so do you."

All of the dialog was directed at me. Digger managed to skate on this one.

Well, there was weeping, wailing, and gnashing of teeth, not to mention a liberal dose of groveling when I went up to Ernie's room. After about a half an hour of pleading and reconciliatory rhetoric, and telling Ernie I would have to drop out of college if he left, he finally agreed to stay with a few conditions.

- There would be no more complaining about the food under any circumstances and I was responsible to convey this message to all employees.
- There would be no more shortages of inventory, especially in the higher priced items, such as steaks, lake trout filets, and pies!
- The clincher in the deal: I promised to get Digger to stop bellowing "**FOOD PLEASE!**" for the rest of the summer.

I asked Ernie, if in light of all the concessions I had made, would he tell The Boss he had decided to stay? Ernie, being a compassionate man, said he would. For the next few days, I avoided The Boss. For about two weeks, I had a terminal case of chapped lips from kissing Ernie's and The Boss's asses.

After the Emp relations with the Concessions hit bottom, the Boss figured he would try to treat everyone with a moonlit cruise and cookout. The cruise was announced with much fanfare; it was to be a trip to Tookers Island next Thursday night.

To say John Haapala was not happy would have been the number one understatement of the summer. When John was told he would be taking the employees on a moonlit boat ride to Tooker's Island, the logic portion of his brain was short circuited. John never stayed up past eight at night, no matter what, and you can't take a moonlit cruise until the Sun sets. Eventually, Sol would give it up around ten, and dip into the water. However, due to the fact that it sets over a hundred miles of water, there is nautical twilight past 11 PM. The best that John could hope for was a one in the morning return.

The Boss was gathering food and picnic supplies for the outing and we had some last minute preparations of our own. Digger's responsibility was to go over to Tooker's and stash two cases of beer in the woods. When we got off work that night, we hit the reserves which were getting dangerously low.

We all had a few beers except Digger, who seemed to be tuning up with more gusto than anyone. We weren't driving, so Digger's theme for the night was "Let her rip." It took two boats to accommodate all of the employees and we finally cast off for the twenty minute ride to Tooker's. We were on John's boat and Oarlocks was piloting the other one.

Digger felt it only fitting and proper that the Emps on the other boat see more than one moon. We formed a semi circle around Digger and based on the howl from the other boat, the extra moon had the desired effect.

It was an accepted fact that Digger was in a mooning league of his own. He had it all: knowing the exact moment to "drop trow" and being agile enough to position the moon to provide the most visibility.

Tooker's Island is about the size of a couple of aircraft carriers with rocks, trees, some grass and a spectacular view of the Harbor on one side and the Big Lake on the other. The lake side of Tookers

Island is mostly a cliff varying in height from fifteen to thirty feet. The full moon made it all the more spectacular.

Everyone pitched in to set the picnic tables, start the fires, and help the cooks get started with food and refreshments. We took a few side trips to partake of our own refreshments.

Whenever anyone passed near Haapala, he would exhort, "Glaze at the moon, boys, glaze at the moon." Haapala figured once everyone had "glazed" at the moon, he could go home.

Digger thought it would be cool to take a piss off the cliff and write his name in the Big Lake. According to Glenn, who was there for the same reason, Digger was weaving some, while searching around for Mr. Happy. Digger tilted back and said, "Get a load of all those stars." I guess that is why the cops have you tilt your head back and touch your nose when they suspect you have been drinking. If you have been drinking, you will lose your balance. Digger flunked the test, big time.

Glenn was hysterical. He sounded like the foreman on the Tower of Babel project. When we finally got him to slow down, we understood Digger took a full gainer off the cliff with Mr. Happy in his hand.

Now WE were worried! A fifteen foot drop unto solid rock sounded ominous even for Digger. We ran to the cliff and sure as hell, there he was, laying stock still on his back, holding Mr. Happy. The waves were gently lapping up to his knees.

Donny knew of another way down to the water and took off. A few minutes later, Donny and I reached Digger.

Digger was peeing before and after impact, so it was hard to tell where on his pants the lake water ended and the recycled beer began. "He's alive!" Donny shouted, almost unbelieving. Donny picked up Digger and started back the way we came. I figured since Donny carried him, it was only fair for me to get Mr. Happy zipped back in before we got back.

After quite a struggle, Donny finally got Digger back to the rest of the party. By this time, everyone knew what had happened and everyone was waiting for us including, The Boss.

About this time, someone suggested we shouldn't have moved him because of potential internal, spinal cord, or back injuries. They obviously were not students of the Bible, or else they would have known God protects idiots and drunks. We had both categories covered.

The way we figured it, Digger must have hit perfectly flat. Even the Bulgarian judge would have given him a 9.5. (The Bulgarians only gave 10s to themselves and the Russians.) I can't think of anyone who attempted any dive with the same degree of difficulty and hit it perfect.

We splashed a little water on Digger's face and he began to come to. His first conscious bodily function was to throw up. We figured about seven beers and a hot dog came out in about one and a half seconds. The girls scattered like a covey of quail. The Boss wondered where and how Digger was able to consume that much beer under tightly supervised conditions.

So much for the picnic. John Haapala, who volunteered immediately, and a contingent, including Donny and me, left to take Digger back while the rest of the Emps carried on half-heartedly. The Boss was not happy. Digger was in the shit house for the next week.

It was my scheduled day off and I figured it would probably be best to make myself scarce. As luck would have it, Kathy had the same day off as I did. I suggested a fishing/hiking day at Chicken Bone Lake.

We left at dawn, which required a boat ride to Chippewa Harbor, some twelve miles from the Lodge. The last two miles are into Chippewa Harbor, which resembles a shrunk down Fjord. We beached the *Sisu* at the end of the Harbor and caught the trail to Lake Richie. When you hike north and south, you are constantly going up or down. Even if you are in shape, this will take its toll.

It is a little over four miles to Lake Richie and it took us about two hours and more effort than I thought. As we rounded the bend on the north end of the lake, we came upon two big tents! As we approached the first tent, a guy that looked like Man Mountain Dean emerged and greeted us with a friendly hello.

He was part of the Park Service trail crew and invited us in for a cup of coffee that was cooking on a four burner, double oven wood stove! That beast must have weighed 400 pounds. Man Mountain Dean didn't wait for the question and volunteered that the trail crew wanted home cooking and carried the stove from the shore where we beached the *Sisu.* He was quick to add that it took them almost all day to get it from the boat to its current location. He almost seemed apologetic.

We told Man Mountain Dean we were headed to Chicken Bone to fish and he said we could catch all the pike we could handle right here at Richie. Kathy and I decided we would end our quest here and went to an opening to cast for northern pike.

The only sound we heard was our lure hitting the water and moments later, the splash of the pike as it resisted being caught. When you are surrounded by one of the greatest trout reserves on the planet, you do not eat northern pike. They are great fighters and resemble fresh water Barracudas. We stopped counting on the number of pike we caught and started back in the afternoon. As we passed the trail guys' tents, Man Mountain Dean invited us to supper. There is no doubt that Kathy was the inspiration for this invitation.

We accepted and the rest of the crew returned from their labors and were almost too happy to see us (Kathy). We had a delicious home made beef stew dinner complete with homemade bread. I offered to share the six pack of Bud I carried in, but they showed me four cases of their own stash and insisted we drink their beer.

I am sure they would have liked us to spend the night, but we started off after supper and made it back to Chippewa at about nine that night. There was still about an hour of sunlight left and we made it back to the Lodge before dark. If this ain't heaven, it's close enough for me.

Chapter 10

REPLENISHING THE SUPPLY (RUM RUNNING)

I was running low on booze, which became a major income source for me. It wasn't easy for an underage kid, sixty miles by water from the nearest liquor store, to get alcohol. Not only did I have alcohol, no one had more than me. The Smokeys presented a major obstacle as they were on an all out vigil, determined to catch me red-handed. They were watching the boats and planes with some regularity. We decided to stop the egg case substitution as there were too many people in on the caper. I could increase the beer supplied from Park Service Headquarters, but booze was another story. No one wanted to be responsible for supplying minors, no matter how hard I tried to sell them on the fact that I was only selling it to tourists to pay my way through college. Besides, no one knew how much I was selling to the tourists, which forced me to go to multiple sources.

One evening I was sitting around lamenting about the dwindling supply and Digger said, "Let's take a run over to Canada. It's cheaper, there are no middlemen, and we can finish our trek across the lake. Remember the Canuck with the Chris

Craft that had us over? He told me to look him up if we ever got over there and he would buy us whatever we wanted."

A Canadian came over from Port Arthur, Fort William and treated Digger, Kathy, and me to dinner on his boat. He ran out of booze during his stay and I sold him a bottle of Canadian Club and a case of Budweiser at cost.

Port Arthur, Fort William was around 40 miles from the Lodge and I never considered going there because it was a foreign country. "Damn good idea," I said even though I had some reservations. It's about 30 miles to the entrance of Thunder Bay from the Lodge, and the water on the north side of the Island always seemed rougher. The old-timers said the comparatively narrow cut between the Island and Canada compressed the winds and currents to create the rough seas.

My other worry was clearing customs, which would leave a trail for authorities to follow. If we couldn't contact our friend, we would have to find a liquor store that would sell to underage foreigners. We would have to transport all of this to our boat and make the return forty mile trip.

Digger reiterated the promise our Canadian friend made to him. Digger guaranteed that he would buy us all the booze we wanted. Since there was no way to contact this individual, he had no idea we would be coming. "What if he was on vacation or out of town for some reason?" I reasoned.

Digger repeated his standard response, "Hell, ya gotta take some chances in this life."

Even though I heard that saw before, Digger could make the improbable seem doable. So, we set out to make our plans. We both arranged for the same day off to go "fishing" on the North Side of the Island. It was set for Wednesday, next week.

On Tuesday, we cornered Glen and told him we were planning to take a run to Canada just for the hell of it. We were leaving that night, and we should be back by noon on Wednesday. If we weren't, he should contact the authorities, as we could be in some trouble. I asked Doc if he would take care of Oarlocks while we were on our "fishing" trip.

We left right after supper and made sure everyone saw us. We packed our fishing gear and headed for Thunder Bay. The lake was fairly smooth and we made pretty good time. Unlike the original crossing, when the Island disappeared, we could see the Sleeping Giant rock formation in Canada. The entrance to Port Arthur/ Fort William was known as Thunder Bay and was to the right of the Sleeping Giant.

At the entrance to Thunder Bay there is a grand lighthouse with a dock capable of accepting ocean going vessels. We tied up the *Sisu* and went up the long ladder to the dock.

I knocked on the screen door of the lighthouse and could see a long table with at least six people sitting down to dinner. A tall, ramrod straight, distinguished man got up and came to the door. If there was a prototype for a lighthouse keeper, he was it.

First, I apologized for interrupting his dinner, and then explained that we were on our way to Thunder Bay for the first time. I asked him if he could give us any tips on getting into the harbor.

We walked down to the dock and he started pointing out landmarks and whether we should steer to the left or right. He then pointed to a buoy and said make sure to stay to the right as there were pilings from an abandoned dock just below the surface.

We thanked him, and it finally dawned on him as he asked, "Where is your boat?"

I pointed down to the *Sisu* and he said, "Where the hell did you come from?'

I said "Isle Royale."

He asked, "When are you going back?"

I replied, "Tomorrow."

He said "There's going to be a hell of a blow tomorrow, and you'll never make it back in that!"

We thanked him for his advice and started back down the ladder. I could still see him shaking his head as we pulled away. We navigated as he instructed and made the final ten plus miles to the end of the bay in darkness. This was always part of the plan, as we didn't want to attract any attention by arriving in daylight. We never had any intention of clearing customs.

We tied up the boat at a vacant dock and started walking toward town. It never dawned on us that someone could have taken the boat if they knew how to operate a pull start on an outboard motor. We were so used to being on the Island; the thought didn't even cross our minds.

We had to go through a large waterfront park, which had an unusual number of people in it for that time of night. We found an old hotel near the park and checked in. We put down a Canadian home address and went to the room to call our Canadian friend, Jerry Garrett.

Jerry was home and very surprised to hear we were in town. He insisted on picking us up and taking us to his house. We had a great time with Jerry and his wife and he reiterated his promise to get us whatever we wanted.

There was one glitch. The Ontario Province liquor stores didn't open until ten in the morning. This would make our noon return to the Island impossible. We did tell Glen to give us a little leeway. Hopefully, he would give us enough.

Jerry picked us up at a quarter to ten and took us to the liquor store. We gave him the money for two cases of Canadian Club whiskey and two cases of Labatt's Pilsner.

On the way to the boat, our host mentioned that the park was full of bums on account of the railroad strike and dock workers strike. He also said if we saw a blue boat with a red diagonal stripe, we should throw all of the booze overboard and surrender immediately. The boat belonged to the Canadian Coast Guard Harbor Patrol.

Jerry dropped us off at the edge of the park behind a big tree and said, "Good luck. You're going to need it."

We have to take some chances. Let's see: we are illegal aliens which calls for instant arrest and jail, we are minors in possession of a large amount of alcohol, we have to somehow get this liquor through one to two hundred bums, evade the authorities on the ground and on the sea, navigate some of the most treacherous waters on the planet, and stash the booze so that the authorities on the Island don't find it. Some chances indeed.

We were standing behind a big tree as Jerry took off, relieved I am sure. As we surveyed the situation, there were bums everywhere, and we had about two hundred yards to go to reach the dock where our boat was tied.

We reluctantly agreed that we could sacrifice the beer if need be. We also agreed that I was the faster runner and in better shape, so I would carry the booze. The plan was for Digger to take off for the far dock carrying a case of Labatt's on each shoulder. I would wait until the bums started after him, and I would try an end around to the boat. If the bums got close, Digger would drop one of the cases of beer and I would pick him up on the other dock.

Digger sauntered out from behind the tree and made for the far dock. A couple of the bums noticed the two cases of beer and I swear I could see them lick their lips. They both got up and started toward Digger. As they got close, Digger let out a war whoop and started running. It was almost like someone rang the dinner bell at the local soup kitchen. All of a sudden, every bum was on his feet and chasing Digger.

Our plan worked so well, it was almost our undoing. I started laughing at the sight of a hundred plus bums chasing Digger to the point where I had to remind myself that we were in a life or death situation. With this sobering thought, I started my end around. It worked to near perfection. A few of the laggards noticed me running with the cardboard boxes emblazoned with Canadian Club across the front and reversed their field and started pursuing me. I had a good head start and the bums were no match, even lugging two cases of CC.

On the other side of the park, the bums were gaining on Digger and he was ridiculing them with bum speak. I made it to the boat, untied the lines and pushed off into the harbor. The bums chasing me were not willing to jump into the forty degree Lake Superior water and I started the engine and headed for Digger's position. Much to my surprise, he was still carrying the beer and running down the dock, calling the bums every name imaginable. I pulled up in the nick of time. Digger jumped in just as the bums were about to attempt a diving tackle. I turned the boat to the center of the harbor, and Digger hurled verbal and visual insults toward the bums standing forlorn on the dock. Digger couldn't resist a parting "moon shot" and I caught a couple bums actually laughing.

We didn't really have a chance to relish our victory over the bums, as we had to start looking for the blue boat with the red stripe. That was the longest fifteen miles I ever traveled from that day to this.

As we neared the lighthouse, with no blue boats in sight, we both decided that it would only be proper to toast the lighthouse keeper with a Labatt's. Our toast was short lived, however, as the prediction of the "big blow" was accurate. As soon as we passed the protection of the small island the lighthouse was on, the wind and waves were on us.

The waves were about six feet, and breaking. Someday, I must write to the Clorox folks and thank them for saving our lives, not once, but twice. Clorox bottles with the ends cut off are the best bailers short of the ones you operate by throwing a switch.

I steered, Digger bailed, and the waves just kept getting bigger.

Back on Isle Royale, Glen was getting nervous. It was two in the afternoon, and we were nowhere. It just so happened that there was a sixty-five foot ocean trawler from the University of Rhode Island charting the bottom of Lake Superior on the north side of the Island. As the boat docked, Glen ran up to the Captain.

"How is it on the north side?" Glen asked.

"Too rough to chart," the Captain answered.

"Do you think you could get through those seas with a fourteen footer?" Glen inquired.

"No way," said the Captain. "The waves are fifteen feet and breaking! No way." he reassured Glen.

Glen knew we would try to get back and since it was almost three PM, he decided to sound the alarm. He ran straight to Jim's office and declared, "Dan and Digger are trying to get back from Canada, and I'm sure they are in big trouble. They were supposed to be back at noon and the Captain of the research boat said it was very rough on the north side."

After he sounded the alarm, Glen told us all hell broke loose. Jim called the Coast Guard and said there was a small boat trying to cross from Canada to Isle Royale. The Coast Guard immediately dispatched a Cutter from Marquette, Michigan, over a hundred miles from Isle Royale. The chance of finding survivors in forty degree waters is very slim, but usually the families are grateful when their loved ones bodies are returned. The Coast Guard also summoned a helicopter from Lower Michigan, more than three hundred miles away.

While this was happening, Digger and I were on the winning end of a case of Labatt's as we took turns bailing. If you consider that we were able to bail at least a half gallon at a clip, we had to have bailed a minimum of three hundred fifty gallons of water out of that boat. At one point, Digger stopped bailing for a brief moment to raise his Labatt's to the sky and proclaim, "Oh Lord, thy sea is so great and my boat is so small."

I just hoped that the Good Lord would take that proclamation in the spirit in which it was intended. Fifteen foot waves in a fourteen foot boat provide everything you can handle. When you are in the bottom of a trough, the only thing you see is a wave coming at you and the one that just passed.

I imagined the tops of the waves looked like the manes of the horses in the song, "Ghost Riders in the Sky." Every time we were sitting in the bottom of a trough, it was hard to imagine that the boat could climb the wall of water coming at us. The waves were the biggest we ever experienced, even counting the ones Dennis and I went out in. We couldn't possibly turn around and our only option was to keep going toward the Island.

There is a big difference between the waves in cold, fresh water and those in the ocean. Fresh water waves are much steeper and closer together. The average depth of Lake Superior between Isle Royale and Canada goes from four hundred to six hundred fifty feet. The water temperature when the lake is stirred up is about forty degrees. The cohesive force of cold fresh water is greater than that of its salt water counterpart.

Thousands of boats have sunk in the Great Lakes due to the close grouping of waves. The largest boat can be pounded into submission. We weren't getting pounded, but the chance of getting "pole pitched" or swamped were real possibilities with every wave.

Any old-timer who spent any time on the Big Lake would

always talk about the "Three Sisters." The Three Sisters were a combination of three rogue waves that lurk in almost all great storms that would test the best boat and crew. These three waves, much bigger than all of the rest, were seen by sailors who told me about them first hand. Whenever there is a sinking on the Big Lake, some old-timer will speculate that they didn't survive the Three Sisters. I kept looking for the triplets and thankfully never had to make their acquaintance.

We were scared, tired and cold. Each wave was giving us a forty degree shower and once again, hypothermia was a possibility. Outrunning bums and bailing cold water for three hours was starting to take its toll.

We didn't know how close we were to the Island, but figured we must have covered some distance during this time. We probably went further up and down than we did going forward. I just happened to look at the six gallon tank between my feet and saw the gauge bouncing on empty! Holy crap! We did bring another tank, but if we shut the engine down to hook up the spare tank, we would surely get turned sideways and capsize.

We would have to disconnect the hose and reconnect it to the full tank while the engine was running. There should be enough gas in the line and squeeze ball to make the switch without turning the motor off, we hoped. I throttled down to the lowest idling speed I could and still keep us going into the waves. Digger switched the hose to the full tank in one quick move and gave the ball a couple of squeezes. The motor sputtered a little but then began its familiar purr.

We returned to the routine of bailing and steering. We finally caught sight of the Island from on top of one of the waves, and Digger, being the expounder of the obvious, declared, "Land Ho." I guessed it was nearing five PM and we both wondered what Glen decided to do.

Finally, we got to the lee side of the Island, and polished off the remaining Labatt's in case number one. Funny how a near-death experience and forty degree water can negate the effects of twelve beers.

I told Digger that we had to stash the stash, in the event of a welcoming party. We pulled the *Sisu* into a small rocky cove, and put the booze and remaining case of Labatt's under a small tree. We covered everything up with branches and headed for Rock Harbor.

As we entered the Harbor, we could see a large contingent on the main dock. There would never be that amount of people on the dock at this time unless a boat was about to tie up, a plane was going to land, or a dignitary was about to visit. Since the answer was none of the above, I guessed they were waiting for us.

Sure enough, the Park Superintendent was on hand to greet us and declared, "Boys, I am going to conduct an inspection of your boat."

"Why would you do that?" I asked.

"Because, you are returning from a foreign land, and this is a customs inspection," he replied.

"But, we are not coming from a foreign country," I declared.

"That is not what Glen told us," the Super said confidently.

"Originally, we did think about going to Canada, but because of the weather, we decided to fish on the North side," I countered. "Besides, no one could have gone through that sea in a fourteen footer and lived to tell about it. And if you need further proof, why not call Canada and see if we cleared customs over there?"

The Super said, "I will do just that. In the meantime, stay right where you are."

He summoned Jim and they went to the Ranger Shack to make the call to Canada and cancel the air and sea search. About

15 minutes later, they returned and by the deflated look on the Super's face, I knew we were in the clear. "You are free to go."

The Super stalked off the dock followed by his lackeys. Jim stayed on the dock until everyone left and he approached me. "Just tell me one thing," he asked. "Did you go to Canada?"

I said, "We sure as hell did, and you're lucky we're still alive."

He looked at me with great astonishment and said, "Why in the hell am I lucky you are still alive?"

"Because, I have a bottle of Canadian Club with your name on it."

"You Sonofabitch, I knew you guys went over there!" was the only thing he could muster. I knew Jim well enough to detect a look of admiration, even while he was giving me hell.

I made good on my promise of a bottle of CC, gave Glen a six-pack of Labatt's, and made the tourists pay for our trip.

Besides, Kathy was also on the dock and she was the best looking welcoming party I ever laid eyes or anything else on.

Chapter 11

LONE TREE ISLAND BECOMES NO TREE ISLAND

Some of our capers were getting back to the Smokeys, which led us to believe there was a rat among us. We figured we could kill two rats with one caper - a real rat and a bureau-rat.

We had enough. We decided the biggest impact would be to make Lone Tree Island into No Tree Island. In the middle of Rock Harbor, a rock thirty foot long and ten foot wide island was home to a single Christmas tree, hence, Lone Tree Island. Its location is much like the Statue of Liberty in New York Harbor. All tourists arriving by boat go directly past Lone Tree.

This is no ordinary tree. It has been there since the 1800's based on test borings made by the Park Service. Lone Tree is the subject of post cards, Smokey lectures, and tourist cameras.

We suspected the rat among us was Freddy, one of the dishwashers. Freddy was good friends with a couple of the Bureaucrat Smokeys and if we were right, all we had to do is let Freddy "overhear" our plan for making Lone Tree Island into No Tree Island.

Digger and I were sitting in the Emp dining room near the dishwashers' station. Freddy was on duty, and Digger said "We ought to show them," and went on to say, "That Kot-Damn tree has lived long enough anyway." By now Freddy was hanging by the door and lapping up every word.

We talked about plans to cut the tree down and pin the deed on Dudley. We would stash a saw under Dudley's steps the night before we cut down the tree. The plan was so stupid, we knew they would fall for it.

We declared a day and then cancelled at the last moment a couple times for trumped up reasons. We were playing havoc with the Smokeys' work schedule as they would cancel all days off to catch us in the act. Finally, we set the deed for Saturday night. It was to be a moonless night and the wind would be calm enough for a landing on Lone Tree Island with tools.

Freddy "happened" to be around when we discussed last minute plans. We would use Donny's boat to get out to Lone Tree because it was painted dark. We would have to stash the boat in Coffee Pot Landing so no one would see us leave Rock Harbor at that time of night. Finally, we had to stash a saw under Dudley's porch Friday night, and cover it with grass and leaves.

Early, on Saturday evening, trying his best not to look conspicuous, Digger left Rock Harbor with Donny's boat loaded with a couple of hand saws and two axes. He could not have been any more conspicuous if he was carrying a stuck-on fog horn while dressed like Bozo the Clown. The Trainee Bureaucrats were taking it all in.

Digger landed in Coffee Pot Landing. I was there to collect the tools and run them back to the maintenance shop. Digger returned with an empty boat, tied it up and we went to supper.

Right after supper, Digger ran Donny's boat down to Coffee Pot Landing and tied it up to a tree. The table was set. All of the Smokeys were assembling in Jim's house and everyone was to take a vantage point to catch us red handed, finally!

Digger and I liberated a six pack from storage and went up on a ridge to watch the Smokeys scramble. They were positioned everywhere - on top of Dudley's roof, Jim's roof, behind the *Ranger III* dock, on the Island across Rock Harbor, and in the bushes behind the old *Ranger II* dock.

The toughest part was not laughing out loud and giving our position away. We sat there for a couple of hours and decided rather than waste any more beer, we would hit the rack. As we snuck through the woods back to the dorm, the Smokeys were still on their all night vigil.

The next morning was an Isle Royale signature day. It was about sixty five degrees, low humidity, slight breeze, and brilliant sunshine. I purposely went down to the gas dock near the Smokey station and hung around with Digger. It wasn't long before Jim came charging out of the Smokey station on a bee line toward Digger and me.

"Good morning, Jim," I said in my cheeriest voice.

"Kiss my ass," was Jim's response.

"Why the grumpiness, Captain Jim?" I asked smiling. "You do look tired." I continued to smile.

"You sonofabitch, you know damn well why I'm mad."

"Well Jim, you should never trust a rat. If they got nothing else to bite, they'll bite you," I counseled.

"I've got a bottle of Jack D with your name on it. That should help you sleep," I attempted to console him.

"Shove it up your ass," Jim replied as he stormed off the dock.

"Keerist, is he mad," Digger offered the obvious.

I hoped I hadn't turned Jim into an adversary. I was convinced that Jim was one of the reasons I was still on the Island.

Digger made another observation. "I am pretty sure we broke every rule in the Smokey manual, but our greatest accomplishment is the fact that they actually made some rules just because of us!"

George still hadn't showed up to reclaim his boat and I used the occasion of Kathy and my day off to take her on a picnic on the other side of the Island. Hopefully, there wasn't anyone else with the same idea.

Our plan was to go to McCargo's Cove which was a long, fairly deep inlet that had a big dock and camping area at the end of the cove. McCargo's is a long way from Rock Harbor on the Canadian side of the Island and even though it is a beautiful spot, it didn't get much use.

It wasn't always that way. Lore had it that during the War of 1812, the British hid a warship in McCargo's cove for most of the war. I can't imagine who they were going to attack on the US side of Lake Superior in 1812. The Yoop was largely uninhabited and copper and iron were yet to be discovered.

Anyone able to live in the Yoop at that time could probably kick the shit out of a boat load of Limies. I believe this was one of those stories told around a campfire many years ago and it just never died.

It was another perfect summer day. Sixty eight degrees felt almost hot when compared against days that didn't get much over forty.

We stopped at Blakes Point to take a couple of passes at our favorite trout spot and we managed to boat a ten pound laker. That would be lunch!

Since George's boat could go like hell, I took a five mile detour off the end of the Island to visit our friends at the Coast Guard Station on Passage Island. We got there about ten thirty in the morning and they were so happy to see us (undoubtedly Kathy more than me), they broke out the beer.

They so seldom got visitors, whenever anyone stopped by, they were thrilled. There are many stories of lighthouse keepers going crazy and even a couple of accounts of them killing their partner. These guys must have pissed off someone in the Coast Guard hierarchy to have landed this duty. Passage Island was one of the most remote manned lighthouses in the lower forty eight.

We cleaned the ten pound laker and had it for lunch with the boys. We shot a little pool, had a couple more beers, and finally shoved off for McCargo's Cove.

There was no one else there. We built a charcoal fire, spread out the blanket on a small patch of grass, and opened a bottle of wine. I couldn't help thinking about Oarlocks definition of heaven and wondering if this wasn't a part of it.

McCargo's is about 3 miles deep and at the end, the water actually warms up in the summer. You can see a boat approaching for miles, so Kathy and I went skinny dipping. Suffer me.

The charcoal was perfect and I cooked the steaks I liberated from the Dock Store.

We shoved off before sunset and figured we would be back at Rock Harbor before dark. I was a little gun shy about boating at night, based on past experience, running lights or not. Besides, it would probably take me ten years to pay back George if anything happened to his boat.

George finally showed up to reclaim his boat. I filled all the tanks to the top and had Jack give him a tune up.

George lifted a floor board and asked what happened to the four cases of beer he had stashed there. I said that three and a half cases pretty much paid for storage and they probably shouldn't drink more than twelve on their trip back to the mainland anyway. In addition, seventy gallons of gas and a tune-up should more than make up for a few beers.

Later that afternoon, we were waiting for the *Ranger III* and Oarlocks was at it again. A tourist showed up with a handful of moose shit. Moose droppings are large green oval trinkets that kinda look like big olives. If they sit for a day or so, they are somewhat solid.

The Toad picked Oarlocks to tell him what they were. Oarlocks asked him, "were they in a clump with a bunch of them?"

The Toad answered in the affirmative.

"Well," Oarlocks began, "those are Isle Royale olives. As soon as they ripen, the vines die and disappear."

I waited for Oarlocks to expound on the taste. Oarlocks must have been in a charitable mood as he told the Toad that although they looked OK, they weren't edible.

He did go on to explain how to tell a female moose from a male moose after the male sheds his antlers. "If you watch them carefully when they browse, the male moose chews clockwise and the female chews counterclockwise," Oarlocks managed to say with a straight face.

I was still pulling the plug for Oarlocks, which became so commonplace, I was able to yank that booger-laden sponge while eating a sandwich. I didn't think Oarlocks was feeling so good. He didn't say anything to me, but being around him as much as I was, gave me a feeling.

The next day, Oarlocks said he was going back to the mainland to have his mouth checked out. The Toad season was winding down anyway and old John could handle the Toads that were left.

There were two more early exits from the Island. It seems Ellen was double-checking her housekeeping staff and found two staff members of the opposite sex were missing. Ellen was a lot of things, but dumb wasn't one of them. She went scurrying back to the Lodge units and started opening doors. My take was that they were just ensuring that the sheets had to be washed.

Ellen screamed the obvious, "What the hell are you doing?"

I will give Dave a couple of points for quick thinking. "We're just necking."

I will give Ellen even more points for her response. "Well, put your neck back in your pants and start packing."

Digger and I decided to try to stay out of trouble and take a "fishing" trip to Duncan Bay. Duncan Bay is around Blake Point on the Canadian side of the Island and pretty much out of the way.

There is very little fishing pressure in Duncan Bay as most boat fishermen go after lake trout or salmon. Duncan Bay has mostly northern pike and perch. What most don't know is that the pike in Duncan Bay are in the trophy category and so are the lowly perch.

We took a five mile detour to visit our Coast Guard buddies on Passage Island. As always, they were glad to see us. There was a world class pool table in the lighthouse and if it wasn't so remote, I couldn't think of a better place on earth to live. Kathy would have to be part of that equation, however.

We shot a few games of pool and we told the boys we were going to Duncan to pick up some perch and maybe a northern or two. They invited us back for a fish fry and some adult beverages on our way home. We always had an open invitation to stay the night if we were over served. We promised to return.

It was a beautiful day on the Island and Duncan Bay is really isolated. We eased into the end of the bay and there among the weeds, we saw a couple of four foot northerns sunning themselves. We offered them every lure in the box, but no bites. We practically dragged the lures over their bodies and still nothing.

It was time for our irresistible lure, an M-80. As I mentioned, an M-80 is roughly equivalent to an eighth stick of dynamite. We taped the M-80 to a rock so it would sink some before going off to help muffle the noise.

Holy Shit! It still made a pretty big bang and some water shot up where I threw it. We waited a minute or so and one of the northern lunkers floated to the surface. I didn't know how to check a northern's pulse, so I didn't know if he was dead or not. Northerns have a million or so teeth that line their mouths, all slanted backwards. This is so when they bite you, you can't pull back without making a hundred blood rows on both sides of your hand.

A northern that big isn't that good to eat, but it is a trophy fish that will give you unlimited bragging rights. Digger had the camera ready, and I reached over to pick the monster up by the gills (with gloves) and hold him long enough for a picture. I almost went out of the boat trying to lift the monster, and finally dragged him over the gunnel into the boat. After humping suitcases and supplies all summer, I was pretty strong, even though I didn't look it. He was at least four feet and although we didn't have a scale big enough to weigh him, I was guessing he went around forty pounds. They are tough to hold as their skin is slimy and this one was pretty limp after kissing an M-80.

Northerns are mostly olive green, with greenish-yellow spots on their body. They don't get a lot bigger than this one.
After Digger snapped the picture, I tossed him overboard and we waited to see if he was KO'd or DOA'd. After a few minutes, he wiggled his tail and slowly swam off.

We knew where the perch hung out, and we couldn't get them to bite either. I taped up a few more M-80's and tossed them in the seaweeds that hid them. The blast liberated several two plus pounders and we threw them in the ice chest. Perch are lowly fish because they are bony and don't yield much edible meat. That is of course unless they are as big as the Duncan Bay perch which have fabulous filets and are among the best fish you will ever taste.

We tossed them in the ice chest and made for Belle Isle. Belle

Isle was a resort in the thirties and was also run by the Knuetsen family. It was probably the most upscale resort on Isle Royale and, as I mentioned before, they actually built a nine hole, par three, golf course there. You could still make out where the greens were because of the nonnative grass growing on them.

We finished a few beers and ate our sandwiches, thenexplored for awhile. I could feel the presence of the tourists at this ghost resort. You could see where the buildings stood, the shuffleboard courts, and the picnic areas. It was an eerie feeling. I got it every time I visited Belle Isle.

It was time to make our way back to Passage Island and share our perch with the United States Coast Guard. The living quarters on Passage were first class. The house was solid stone and could have taken a direct hit from "Little Boy" or "Fat Man."

We had a fabulous fish fry and shot pool into the wee hours. We never had any intentions on going back to Rock Harbor that night. I wonder what the Coast Guard regulations said about us yahooing at the lighthouse.

The boys told me to come back soon, sooner if Kathy was with me. We made it back to the Lodge in time to take a shower and start our daily routine.

I bought a fifty dollar money order from Dennis and sent Piggy the last payment for the motors. I put a note with the payment and said as far as I knew, we were square; if his accounting didn't agree, let me know. I never heard a word from Piggy.

One of the housekeeping guests flagged me down and asked if I could clean some fish for him. Since we pretty much did everything, I agreed. He had two ice chests full of trout and as near as I could count, there were over fifty of them. What a way to spend an afternoon: up to your elbows in fish guts. It took three days to wear off the fish smell. The guy tipped me three bucks. It is Lurch's turn.

A housekeeping guest had a huge fifty-five horsepower motor on the *Ranger III* dock that he just got repaired, and wanted to get it to his boat in Tobin Harbor. He offered me five dollars to get it over the hill and down the steep, rocky trail to the boat docks in Tobin Harbor. I took the five and said I would get it there within the hour.

I was waiting for Lurch to show up as we had to unload supplies from the *Ranger III.* When he got there, I said I would bet him a buck he couldn't run that motor to the number two dock in Tobin without stopping. He bit. He ran with the motor on his shoulder so fast, I could barely keep up. He set the motor on the dock and I promptly handed him the dollar.

Chapter 12

FAREWELL TO ARMS

(With Apologies to Ernest Hemingway)

Ned needed help with the gas we stored on the Island earlier. The fifty-five gallon drums of aviation gas were stored on a hill behind the dorm and incinerator. What a dandy fire that would have been! There were still only a few of us that knew about the gas barrels.

Ned had to use it up before he made his last trip. So, we went up with ten five gallon cans and hand pumped it from the barrels into the five gallon cans. We had a funnel with a screen to make sure there were no chunks getting into the *Goose*'s gas tanks.

There was quite a bit of water in the barrels and it looked like the screen was catching it. We had to dump the water from the funnel fairly often. Ned wasn't concerned. After filling the five gallon cans, we had to carry them down a rocky hill to the dock, load them in the NPC wooden scow, and pour them into the wing tanks on the top of the *Goose*.

The Pratt and Whitney's seemed to miss more on start up than before. I didn't fly back with him on any of those trips.

Against all odds, our resident duck, Herman, survived through the summer and defied the seagulls to try to get him. He was almost as big as a seagull and had only one disadvantage. He couldn't fly. I guess flying is something he would have been taught by his parents. I am pretty sure we could have picked him up and thrown him in the air into the wind, but we worried he wouldn't know what to do. He never did see another duck like himself and he didn't dare wander out of the security of Snug Harbor.

He watched some of the other birds heading south. They were mostly geese and even though Herman had no formal education, he knew he had to leave the Island.

One day, I saw Herman flapping his wings for all they were worth to no avail. All he did was roil the water. The next day, he did the same thing, but he did move forward, although he still didn't get airborne. The third day, he actually managed to fly about six feet over the water and was enjoying himself until he realized he didn't know how to land. He just folded his wings and did a belly flop. I thought about Howard Hughes and the Spruce Goose.

We were loading the *Ranger III* with the last batch of Lodge tourists and we were all concerned about Herman catching on with a flock of his own heading south. Herman was circling Snug Harbor as he did everyday for the past week. It seemed like he was doing it for our benefit. This was the first time we saw Herman fly over the *Ranger III* and he made several passes. We were all waiting for the *Ranger III* to arrive with the last batch of tourists for the summer and Herman used the gathering to his advantage. He took off, circled all of us twice, and climbed into the clear blue sky heading south. No, there wasn't a dry eye among us, but we knew Herman would thrive and possibly be back. Any duck that could survive the attack of the seagulls was one tough son of a bitch. As I watched him disappear into the sky, I was thinking that not only was he tough, but he was also one super smart duck. I hoped he would have a bunch of ducklings someday.

Sam walked into the Emp dining room at dinner and said he had some bad news: Oarlocks had terminal cancer and wasn't going to make it. There was complete silence and some of the girls were crying. I was trying not to, but it wasn't working. I left dinner and went back to my room. I would have loved to hear him snore one more time.

The only way I could cope at this time was to write Oarlocks a letter:

Dear Oarlocks,

Sam told us of your situation and everyone here is praying and hoping you are as good as you can be.

I couldn't help thinking about the experiences we all shared with you and if I could turn back the clock, I would and …

… fire up the guest house fireplace, get all the Emps around to listen to the warning about oarlocks

… sit around the Emp dorm and watch the girls as you told them about the different aspects of heaven, especially the part where there is 40 acres of tits that squirted scotch and soda

… watch you give the tourists an informal lecture on how all of the outer islands were placed there in WPA days

… see those northern lights from the old "Ranger III" dock knowing there is no greater light show except on the North Pole

… watch the Rock Harbor Lodge buildings come into view from the bow of the "Isle Royale Queen" and get the sensation that you are about to land on a magical place

> ***... sit on a dock in Tobin Harbor and while casting for a lunker, listening to the call of the resident loon ... load your boat with Emps and go to Tookers Island for a cookout and have Digger moon Haapala's boat to everyone's delight except Haapala (I might change the part where Digger took a full gainer off the cliff)***

Well Oarlocks, all of us have seen and done those things. I see them still. Hope your memories are the same. May God bless and keep you.
All of Us, especially Me.

We got word from the mainland. Oarlocks didn't make it. Somewhere there is a 40 acre field of tits squirting scotch and soda and one happy Oarlocks.

With the passing of Oarlocks, Digger and I went fishing on Blake Point and began waxing nostalgic. Again, it was one of those picture-perfect, late summer days. There wasn't a cloud in the sky which is pretty unusual on the Big Lake.

We stopped at one of our favorite reefs that extended off the end of the Island and the conditions could not have been more perfect. Because of the lack of wind and current, we pretty much stayed in one place. We could see rocks and fish on the bottom and we dropped a weighted line. The bottom we could see was fifty feet down!

We fished with frozen smelt chunks and sinking Rapalas. The lakers were hitting everything we offered. As I was reeling in an eighteen pounder and sipping a Bud between reeling and the fish running, I couldn't help thinking out loud, proclaiming, "Ya know Digger, these are the best days of our lives, but at least we had 'em." We lost track of time, which can happen when the fish are biting and daylight does not diminish.

As the sun approaches the horizon on the Island, one is struck by the brilliance. There aren't many places on earth where the sun is as bright on the horizon as it is in the middle of the sky. Even in a forested wilderness, there is a haze given off by the trees which diminishes the suns brilliance as it approaches the horizon.

The sun was nearing the horizon and at Blake Point, we had an unimpeded view of the sun setting in the west. The enormous fire ball was about to be extinguished by the Big Lake and the sight of the sun entering the water was spectacular. The Big Lake was almost dead calm and looked like a freshly ironed sheet as it is settling on a bed when you make it. The color of the water changes with whatever it reflects and this evening it was a spectacular blue. And to think you could still dip your cup and take a drink!

Hopefully, that sight and this day will be the last thing to leave my memory.

Digger and I reviewed the bureaucrat ball busting scorecard and decided it was time to let them spend their last few weeks on the Island without looking over their shoulders. We agreed that we would sponsor a small party with Jim and his direct reports. Since the NPS twits were all over twenty one, liability wasn't an issue.

As soon as we got back to the Lodge, I looked up Jim and issued the invite. Jim said he would make the Smokey lodge available complete with fire. He added that he was pretty sure the chimney would not experience a back up.

Jim said he would provide the refreshments since a good amount was ours in the first place. The only people invited were the Smokeys from our end of the Island, Digger, Dennis, and me.

The party was almost a love fest compared to the prevailing mood all summer. We wished each other well and discussed plans after the Island gig. I did notice on one trip to the bathroom that Dudley had removed all personal toiletry items.

It was time for my last cookout with Kathy. I had Digger select a couple of steaks and I was able to bribe the third cook, Doc, to bake a couple of potatoes, make a salad, and strawberry shortcakes.

I borrowed the folding card table from the Guest house along with a couple of folding chairs and took them out to Scoville point and set them up on a flat spot, complete with a checkered table cloth, plates, and silverware. I hid a couple of bottles of wine in the bushes and went back to shower and pick up Kathy.

I put on my Hathaway shirt, wax hide loafers, cuff-less slacks, and waited on the employee dorm steps for Kathy. When she came down the steps, it looked for all the world like Vivien Leigh in *Gone with the Wind*! Holey moly, she was dressed to the nines and looked like a movie star. We went up the back trail to the *Sisu* which was provisioned and set to go.

To say Kathy was surprised when she saw the table set up like a restaurant, complete with candles, would be an understatement. I also had a couple of inflated air mattresses to "relax" on between courses.

The next event convinced me once again that the angels were looking out for me for reasons I never understood. The sun had set and there was no moon this night. At first the northern lights started out like a green fire dancing on the northern horizon. We must have dozed off for a while and when we woke up, the northern lights covered the entire sky! At the very center of the sky, there was a black circle from which all of the northern lights seemed to emanate from. If there was a Guinness record for kissing, we probably broke it.

I didn't care if I ever got back, but as the sun began to rise, we packed up what we could get into the boat and headed for the Lodge. Bummer.

Our last day was fast approaching and we began closing the

housekeeping cabins and two of the Lodge units. The maintenance guys were scheduled to stay for a few weeks later than the rest of us.

I made one last stop in Tobin Harbor to see if I could catch the resident lunker brook trout. As I sat on the dock, the Tobin loon was yodeling louder than ever; his woeful cry was echoing off the Greenstone Ridge. "oo-AH-ho" with the middle note higher, followed by a "kee-a-ree, kee-a-ree" with the middle note lower. [1] Add to that the sun setting in an array of red streaked clouds and I knew there are few places and times I would ever witness beauty like this again.

The LAST DAY finally arrived. Everyone was walking around like someone just shot their dog. Tomorrow was the day everyone was scheduled to go back on the *Ranger III.* I was walking along the finger docks and realized the *Sisu* was gone! I ran into Woody and he was smiling like the proverbial Cheshire cat. "Missing something?" Woody asked.

"Don't suppose you know anything about my boat?" I offered.

Woody turned around and pointed to the deck of the *Ranger III.* There on top, was the *Sisu* which was commandeered by Woody's crew.

"You're coming home with me." Woody confirmed. "Understand that the stunt you pulled is a once in a lifetime deal. That's because most times your lifetime ends there."

With one more night on the Island and no boat, I used one of the Concession scows and took Kathy to Lookout Louise for one last outing. Lookout Louise overlooks Canada and you can see the lights of Port Arthur, Fort William, and a rock formation called the sleeping giant.

---

1 Loon call description from *National Audubon Society® Field Guide to North American Birds*

We caught a northern light show that paled in comparison to the one we saw the night before and headed back to the boat. We had one last kiss on the Tobin Harbor dock and headed for the dorm.

The last day was upon us and it seemed like we just got there. As I was packing my bags and emptying my dresser drawers, I found a knife wrapped in a note. It read, "I wanted you to have this knife so you would always have something to remember me by. Thanks for all your help, and watch out for those oarlocks!" The knife was Oarlocks Buck knife and he never went anywhere without it. I went into the bathroom and cried.

I waited on the back steps for Kathy and she came down carrying her suitcase. She asked me why my eyes were all red and I showed her the knife and note. She cried.

We threw our stuff on the luggage cart and headed for the dining room for our last breakfast. I noticed there was more than one Emp with red eyes at breakfast.

The boss came in and said a few words thanking all of us for the successful summer and wishing us well. I showed him the note and the knife and caught him wiping a tear from his eyes.

It was a beautiful September day and we got on the *Ranger III* for the seven and a half hour ride home. Kathy and I sat on the fantail and watched the Lodge disappear. We knew each other's plans for the winter, but Kathy asked if I would reconsider going back to school and instead join her in Vail. I said that is all I had been thinking about for the last few days.

We sat holding hands and people would come by to exchange names and numbers. We finally docked in Houghton and my parents and little sister were waiting. As we walked down the gang plank, I noticed my sister hiding behind my Mother, sticking her tongue out at Kathy. I promised Kathy we would take her to the airport for the flight back to her home in Kansas.

They put the *Sisu* on my neighbor's trailer and the Headquarter boys said I could leave it there for a few days until I could tow it home.

I was feeling numb and can't remember what I said when I kissed Kathy goodbye at the airport. It was like falling off a mile high cliff.

Ned asked Digger and me if we would like to fly back to Florida with him. Let's see, a two thousand mile trip in a World War II Grumman *Goose* to warm weather for a week or so. Sounds like another adventure for the Yooper Boys.